Playing House

Playing House

Patricia Pearson

AVON
TRADE

An Imprint of HarperCollins*Publishers*

HarperCollins books may be purchased for education, business, or sales promotional use. For information please write: Special Markets Department, HarperCollins Publishers Inc., 10 East 53rd Street, New York, NY 10022.

FIRST EDITION

Designed by Elizabeth M. Glover

Library of Congress Cataloging-in-Publication Data

Pearson, Patricia, 1964–
    Playing house / Patricia Pearson.—1st ed.
        p. cm.
    ISBN 0-06-053437-0
    I. Title.

PS3616.E26P55 2003
813.'6—dc21

2003049920

03 04 05 06 07 JT/RRD 10 9 8 7 6 5 4 3 2 1

For Ambrose,
and in memory of Mary Ann Duffy

New life announces itself as a mystery that a mother cannot solve. Something happens, a certain gear-shifting in the body that she notes, but makes no sense of. Especially if she isn't planning to be pregnant. I shall offer myself as an example. I did not have a basal thermometer handy on my bureau, or any recall as to when I last had my period. I was not expecting to read *What to Expect When You're Expecting*. I was barely even in a relationship, with a man about whom I knew little. I was simply going about my business, enjoying early spring in New York City, when all of a sudden I woke up in the clean morning sunshine to find that my breasts had inflated like dinghies and were heavier than my head.

Late for work, I fiddled with my bra straps irritably, to no avail. They had all the supportive power of Scotch tape. I searched through the clothes on the floor of my one-room apartment and dragged on a shirt taut with Lycra, then I cupped my breasts in my hands as I stepped gingerly down the four flights of stairs of my walk-up, arranging my arms just so—as I entered the brisk-stepping crowds on Sixth Avenue—so that I could look like I was clutching myself in vexed contemplation over the Great Issues of the Day, as opposed to holding my tits up.

My first assumption was that I had a bad bout of PMS, so I dosed myself with evening primrose oil. We were wrapping up our April issue at *The Pithy Review,* heading into the inevitable panic of magazine production. There were last-minute changes, troubles with ad placement, authors to placate after pompous sentences were slashed from their essays, an editor-in-chief who rendered himself inaccessible behind closed doors in a pointed sulk. It happened every month, as if none of us possessed a short-term memory.

I had, myself, a rant to scribble for the back page, which I'd put off until the last minute, and a half-finished play to complete by the first of April. There was a letter to be sent to the editor of *The New York Times* about the treatment of carriage horses in Central Park, and postcards home to be mailed, lists of ideas, Post-it notes about people to meet, cocktails and beet chips to consume at the Temple Bar.

Life in a city as opportunistic and exuberant as New York always felt busy, even if nothing got done. It was the whirl of the place, the sense of movement that mattered to me, and I grounded myself with small certitudes: I am here. I pay my rent. I like my friends. I have a membership to MOMA. God, when I think about it now, what a slender ledge of a life I was comfortably sitting on then.

On Good Friday, I was in Rizzoli's bookstore contemplating the new Sylvia Plath biography, when I realized that my nipples were so sensitive that I couldn't turn around quickly without crying out. For a few days, I donned the softest fabrics I could find in my closet—an old cashmere sweater my mother had given me to coddle myself through a documentary on Kurds, a silk blouse, and double-wired bra to ineffectually brace me for dance lessons—and still I walked around going, "Ow, ow, ow," as if I'd fallen into a patch of nettles.

Perplexed, I peered at myself in my small bathroom mirror, which entailed leaning over sideways while standing on the worn enamel sides of my tub, effectively looming into the circular looking-glass from stage left. My breasts looked more or less the same as always. My nipples seemed darker, and even bigger, somehow, but I hardly ever looked at my breasts. I liked my waist and my rear end, but in truth my breasts grew in a bit droopy from the outset, with the nipples too low on the orbs, as if Mother Nature stuck them on during a game of pin the tail on the donkey. I had a tendency to fling my arms above my head like the Venus de Milo whenever lovers were afoot, in order to lift the nipples to a more acceptable position. It took a bit of work, this maneuver, especially when I had to walk across the room to answer the phone. But worth it, you know, for not revealing everything your nakedness actually offers to say.

I'd been arm lifting quite a bit of late, because of a fellow named Calvin Puddie. No. Pudhee. Or no, that doesn't look right—I think it could be Puhdey. In any event, it's some sort of French Canadian name, or more specifically Acadian, as in the French who emigrated to eastern Canada, and otherwise to Louisiana.

"That strikes me as a rather stark pair of choices," I told Calvin on our second date. "Either they opted for the frozen, craggy coast of Cape Breton and slogged away in coal mines, or they got to do Mardi Gras? A or B?"

"Well, it's a bit more complicated than that," he said lightly. But being a rather laconic man, he chose not to elaborate.

I knew that Calvin's father was a coal miner, and that he himself had been aiming no higher than a job as a janitor at the local veterans' hall when someone pointed out that he was musically gifted and ought to pursue it. This inspired him to head to Halifax to study music, after which he moved to Toronto, and from there, at some point, to New York. He worked as a jazz musician, living off the avails of his art, which was the annual salary equivalent of two Smarties and a piece of string.

We met at a bar called the Knitting Factory, where a band was playing Indonesian gamelan music. It was something a friend had dragged me to, and that friend bumped into Calvin, whom he knew through a mutual friend, who was a friend of other friends. So various friends gathered, and obediently listened to the occasional *ping* followed by half an hour of murderous silence, as is the tradition in gamelan music, and my friend from work said, "Frannie, that guy over there is also Canadian."

Therefore you must meet him, because you are of the same nationality.

So, after several vodka tonics, I did, and he was funny, if quiet. Very, very quiet, really, bordering on mute. He sat there in an old fedora with his hands placidly in his lap, gazing around inscrutably, tapping his brogues on the floor as if absently filling in rhythmic gaps for the musicians on stage.

He reminded me of Canada in small, distinct ways. His self-effacement was familiar, and he understood certain expatriate secrets, such as where Alberta was and how it felt to be treated like a doofus in Manhattan for being Canadian, as if we were a nation of cheerful, unimportant people with Down's syndrome.

He also had a talent for sly ridicule, which I happily discovered before I left the premises and forgot all about him. There was a novelist in our party who had had too many favorable notices in *The Paris Review* to keep his head low. He began droning on at length about anthropology and American Indians, whom he'd researched for an upcoming novel called *Whiskey Lament*. With his chin up and tilted in faux-reflectiveness, ennobled by his whitey-pants guilt, he waxed eloquent about Big Bear and Running River and Dances With Wolves, until I waned, bored senseless. I wanted to leave and began to pull on the sleeves of my jacket, tugging futilely until I realized that one of them was inside out. Calvin had been watching me, and tipped his fedora up an inch: "Calling it a night, Struggles With Coat?"

We began hanging out. Not really dating, as such, but meandering through the city in comfortable silences and chuckling at store signs, such as the one he pointed out in Chinatown that advertised BEAUTY. RICE. AIDS.

"Beauty you have," he offered to me gallantly. "AIDS you don't wish to acquire. But it would be my pleasure, madam, to buy you your own sack of rice."

One night, after draining all the alcohol in my apartment, he came over to my narrow single bed and climbed in beside me. I kicked and shooed sleepily, "No." I pressed my face into his collarbone. He hugged me and lay still: never mind. But you know how it is, how eventually your loneliness strips you. After a few more walks, more films, more lunches on Sunday, he began to sleep over, to warm me with his unassuming presence. He understood the rules of courtship in our generation: touch without faith, suppress all expressions of hope as bad manners. Do what we're doing, pretend that we're not.

And then this puzzling something happened. This highly unexpected mischief with my breasts.

After a lengthy exam in the bathroom mirror, I switched off the light and wondered, in awesome testimony to the power of denial, if I'd simultaneously developed eczema and put on weight.

"Do you think I'm fat?" I asked Calvin, when we talked on the phone that night. We were having one of those sweet, aimless conversations you get to have when you're newly interested in somebody and have nothing important to discuss.

"No," he said, amused. (This sort of question has a charm half-life of about two weeks. After that, the man tends to interrupt tersely when you're partway through the sentence. "Do you think I'm f—" "Late. Gotta go.")

For now, he was still thinking: *Silly, charming girl.* So I basked in his permission to pose worried little queries.

"I think my breasts have gained weight."

"All right, just lower them carefully onto the scales from a sitting position and then advise them on their diet."

"What if I weighed four hundred pounds, would you leave me?"

"Yes." He said this wryly, just playing along.

"What if I left you? Not when I weighed four hundred pounds, but this month, what if I left you?"

"I'd join the foreign legion."

How romantic! How untrue!

The next day I barfed into a sweater display at the Gap. Surely, I should have known it wasn't the seafood bisque I had just eaten at the Time Café? Seafood generally agreed with me, as did pinot grigio, three espressos, and a couple of bites of gingerbread. Indeed, I felt fine when I ducked into the Gap on my way back to work on West Broadway, and was just investigating a new pair of jeans, thinking to myself that it would be a vast improvement in my ability to be fashionable if flared pants did not begin their flare at precisely the height I have to hem them, when all at once my mouth began to water and I broke into a sweat. My stomach lurched, I darted frantically toward nowhere in particular and ran head-long into the sweaters, which I proceeded to ruin in one commodious heave.

Shocked, I raised my head slowly from my dripping hand and dared to peer around the store. Is everyone staring at me? Why yes, they are! The salesclerk was a few feet away, frozen in midstride, regarding me with the wide-eyed solemnity of Agent Scully encountering an alien.

Oh. I'm so sorry.

"You wouldn't have a napkin or a Kleenex, by any chance?"

How about a mop?

I cleared my throat as discreetly as I could, and went off to commit suicide in the fitting room.

What this meant about my life—including my ability to ever fit into any of the ten sweaters I had to purchase (*you vomit, you pay*) from the white-lipped clerk—remained stubbornly opaque to me. In novels and films, women always seem to discover they are pregnant by feeling faint and having to quickly sit down with the blush draining out of their cheeks. It was romantic, suggesting fragility and need of a gentleman's rescue. That was my notion.

This was not that.

"Do not, under any circumstances, go near the seafood bisque at the Time Café," I therefore told my friend Marina when I got back to the office. "Of course you wouldn't, since you're a vegan," I added. "But warn your friends. You will not believe what I just did."

Marina was going to be the star of my one-woman play, but in the meantime she acted as the receptionist at *The Pithy Review,* a job she attended to with a grim, self-loathing competence. She was smart enough to be the editor-in-chief. But she didn't have the résumé, having flung herself like a June bug at the lights of Broadway for ten years after majoring in theater in college. Her valiant theatrical ambition got her one gig as an understudy in an off-Broadway play that collapsed after opening night. Now here she was, at thirty-five, with nothing on paper to prove her quick and literate mind. She was a fine-boned, green-eyed beauty, but her expression most days was one of deep exasperation.

I had just finished my barf-in-the-Gap yarn when the Great Editor himself padded into the reception area with a Marlboro dangling from his lips. He was, as usual, in his stocking feet, since his wood-paneled office lined with books was more his home than home itself, and of course there were all sorts of rumors about that. But he was otherwise elegantly turned out in a dark green suit and pale gold tie, having gone out to lunch with the director Anthony Minghella.

"Marina," he rumbled in his bass voice, not quite looking at her while he sheepishly held up an apple, "when you have a moment, there are bits of white wax on my apple that I can't seem to rub off. Perhaps you'd do a better job . . ."

Marina glared at him. "Just stick it in my *in box.*"

The Editor actually did so, to our vast bemusement, and then turned his sidelong attention to me. "Frannie, I gather the Joyce Carol Oates story has come in, so I'd like you to have a look today, if you can. I don't want to inadvertently repeat any of her metaphors in my own essay." I nodded obediently and he padded off silently, trailing smoke.

"Do I smell like vomit?" I asked Marina.

"Not yet," she replied, and turned to attend to the complaining phone.

I headed down to my cubicle—a washroom-sized space with a desk and an off-kilter chair—and began to flip through the Oates manuscript, rolling my pencil contentedly back and forth between two fingers. I love editing. I love the precision of it, and the focus. It stills me. I enter the minds of the finest thinkers of our time as if through a secret passage and polish their thoughts. Clarifying a concept here, querying a word there. I consider myself a craftswoman, or even a sculptress. I can't think my way out of a cab for having to calculate the tip, but I can edit. Yes I can! Sometimes, when I'm drunk, I proclaim that I am the power behind the throne, like William Shawn at *The New Yorker*. A founder of intellectual empires. A leader of sock-footed men. *En garde!* We are musing!

When I'm standing in line at a shop, I confine myself to fuming about the businessmen ahead of me, and imagine bursting out—*rat-a-tat*—like The Lone Semantic: "*Psychologize* is not a fucking word!"

The afternoon slipped by as I contemplated the sequence of sentences, every now and then reaching down to rustle my hand in a potato-chip bag, until I realized that I'd eaten the whole lot. I poked my head into the next cubicle and mooched some blue corn chips. Then I resumed, snacking and editing and snacking long into the quiet night.

The next morning, I was heading up West Broadway to work when I suddenly got blown over sideways by a thunderous clamor in my head to eat a bowl of mashed potatoes.

"Eat mashed potatoes with gravy *right now.*"

I looked around, unsure where the voice had come from. Not me, surely? I'd never had the faintest interest in mashed potatoes with gravy.

And now look. What's this? I'm storming into a diner and waving away the proffered menu—"Nope, thanks, know what I want."

I wanted to go on a gobbling spree all over Manhattan.

After several days of this, I realized that I had to talk to myself in that mirror. Leaning sideways, staring sternly into my own brown eyes, I said: *Look here, Frannie, you're running about with a feverish lust for gravied mashed potatoes, preferably accompanied by a tuna salad sandwich. And a Rice Krispies square. And a packet of almonds. And chocolate milk. And another Rice Krispies square. And some peas.*

Jolly Green Giant. Love of my life, fire of my loins . . .

You can't, by any chance, be pregnant?

Never Tell a Man Your Age

April 21, 1999

<u>TO DO</u>

    Marina b-day party at Gramercy Tavern
    Lawyer re: H-1 visa
    Check serial killer trial date, sked piece
    Cronenberg retrospective: Calvin/Susan
    Pee on stick. Blue?

"Do you wanna grab a bite?" Calvin asked me the next night, calling from the bar where he'd been setting up his drum kit for a gig.

"I'd love to, yeah," I said, wincing as my nipple glanced off the phone cord. "I'm starving. They don't have Rice Krispies squares at the Ear Inn, do they? On the dessert menu?"

"I have not noted that on their menu, no." He said this with pleasure in his voice. He liked it that I come out of nowhere sometimes. Calvin favored women who are slightly off-center, which wasn't surprising, given that he was an experimental jazz musician who had been known to play, among other instruments, a balloon and an electrified rake.

Of course, he had no idea that I was a live grenade about to come winging onto the stage to blow up his percussion ensemble forever, and I wasn't going to tell him, because I didn't have the nerve.

It was a fine evening for April, unusually balmy, and in spite of the path I was trodding down, I walked along Sixth Avenue with a spring in my step, for I was carrying within me this sense of miraculous secret. Me? A goddess of maternity? Oh, go on. I never.

It was a sentiment entirely unanchored in the facts, which were deeply alarming. But the air was stirring and alive, and for now I allowed myself this relieved sense of surrender. After all these years, all the pregnancy scares, month after month of staving conception off with a pitchfork and a torch and a battalion of unpleasant contraceptives, fighting the good fight of not making men feel *obliged,* or anything, to be in a committed *relationship,* or anything, and here I'd thrown up my hands. "Okay, I surrender, God, knock me up!"

A woman came trundling toward me, pushing a baby carriage. I smiled softly. You? Me? Same club. She smiled back, a little tiredly, blowing her breath upward to riffle her unkempt bangs. "Nice night, huh?"

"Not bad," I agreed. Her baby, lost somewhere within the confines of a bunting bag, began a small, insistent mewling. I imagined leaning in and fishing around in the bag to pick the infant up and sing to her softly. All that came to mind was a Jethro Tull song I'd heard on the radio that day. "Aqua lung my friend . . ."

I slowed my stride in dismay, patting at the pockets of my red suede coat in search of a cigarette. I can't have a baby, *What am I thinking?* The facts came stampeding into my brain. Single! Busy! Don't know songs! Very small apartment, very, very small.

These were straws that couldn't bear the weight of my predicament, I understood that. I couldn't have a baby, but on the other hand, I did, apparently, have a baby, and I couldn't *not* have this particular baby, because I was thirty-three, and what baby, exactly, was I planning to have? Children had always fit into my sense of the future, however abstractly, and here one was. Unexpected, to be sure, but already obstreperously announcing her presence at life's ball.

So on I walked, happy/terrified all the way down into SoHo, across Spring Street in the shadow of warehouses, absorbed in a kind of mental peekaboo with the reality within me until I reached the Ear Inn, a hole-in-the-wall pub that beckoned warmly in the swiftly chilling dark.

Calvin was waiting at a table with his customary pint of Double Diamond, contentedly scanning the crowd. His nut-brown hair was all askew. That was his trademark, uncombed hair that leaped about like waves, with one lock sweeping downward to obscure a deep-set, blue-green eye. He was wearing a black T-shirt with a picture of a band called The Residents on it, which is to say an eyeball sporting a top hat, and over that a black dress shirt, unbuttoned. One hand was drumming on the gingham tablecloth.

He smiled as I sat down, with a look that was welcoming and expectant. I immediately felt defensive: *Don't get fresh with me, Mister . . . Whoever You Are.* As if he'd gone ahead and arranged our marriage with the village elders when I still hadn't made up my mind. To dodge his affections, I reached for the crayons that the Ear always kept on its tables jammed into juice glasses, and began to doodle squares and diamonds on the paper place mat.

"How was today?" he asked.

"All right," I ventured. There was no point telling him I'd narrowly averted throwing up some peas on the subway, since the very blue stick from my pregnancy kit remained verboten conversation. He sensed a bit of turmoil and tried to cheer me up. "How are your breasts doing on their diet?"

"Fine." I smiled, in spite of myself.

"Got them on soy sauce and kale? Or the other one, that protein thing, Frank did it. All he had for two months was beef and cigarettes, as far as I could tell."

"You don't want to know what I've been eating," I muttered. I glanced at him and noted in horror that his lips were too thin. He nodded hello to Frank, who sat slouched at the dark wooden bar. Then he leaned over and whispered, "Frank wants to kick Lily out of the quartet." The band he was playing with tonight was an improv ensemble featuring Dobro, marimba, saxophone, and assorted appliances. Frank was the sax player; he looked rather melancholy there at the bar, with his graying hair pulled into a thin ponytail. He gazed morosely into a glass of bourbon. Lily was the guitarist. "She plays out of tune," Calvin explained, "and none of us can get her to hear it. I'm amazed she's been on the scene for this long without anyone sending her back to square one to do scales."

I nodded noncommittally, uncertain how "tune" factored into Calvin's music.

"Frank doesn't want her to come with us to Europe," he added. The Garden Snakes were shortly about to set off for an extended tour of hash bars and park rondelles in Holland, Germany, and Austria. The Europeans seemed to love this sort of jazz, whereas to me it sounded like the soundtrack you might hear in a film documentary about dung beetles. Each musician appeared to wander off in a different direction in a spooky, aimless way, and just when a melody surfaced, seemingly inadvertently, out came the balloon or the comb or the electrified windshield wipers or something. The jazz aficionados who crowded into these gigs always listened intently with their lips parted in half smiles, while I looked hopelessly baffled.

I hesitate to think of myself as musically daft, but I do

tend more toward pop melody. Sometimes, in the dead of night when absolutely no one is stirring, I hum a Phil Collins song from 1985. *Da da something, shining in the night, oh lord, uh-huhuh.* I have had to conceal this very carefully from Calvin lest he fall over and die of a heart attack.

"Would you like a beer?" he asked.

"Why not?" The waiter brought me a Double Diamond. I pondered it dubiously. I supposed that I shouldn't be drinking. Curious how something so benign a month ago was now, for all intents and purposes, a stein of toxic waste. What if I forgot not to drink? I suddenly worried. What then? Pregnancy doesn't give you much time to reconfigure your lifestyle. Calvin excused himself to go outside with Frank, where they smoked one metric ton of pot before taking their places at the front of the bar. I pushed the beer aside and concentrated on stuffing myself, doodling on the place mat, wondering how adoption agencies worked, and watching Calvin perform. His head lolled and dipped as he banged on miscellaneous percussive instruments with a variety of sticks and brushes. His eyes were closed; his mouth hung slack. He looked a bit stuporous. I wondered if this were musical ecstasy, as he insisted, or if he'd actually gotten too high and was shortly going to fall off his stool.

The Heart and
Its Insufferable Wants

"What have I done, hooking myself up with Calvin?" I demanded of Marina the next day, as the two of us sat in Washington Square Park with take-out lunches, enjoying the gentle sunlight.

"I have no idea," she said, poking at her tofu with chopsticks. "He certainly isn't your type."

A man sporting a rubber dog nose glided by us on a unicycle. Pigeons pecked and puttered at our feet. Somewhere a couple were arguing in strident voices, and from across the park, more distantly, came the plucky twang of a banjo.

"No, he isn't my type. He's too calm."

"He's pretty quiet," she agreed. "He's not glamorous, and he lets you overshadow him, but I think that's good."

"I know, it probably is good, but I'm not used to it. There's no tension there, he's more like a friend."

"Maybe you need a friend," Marina said, offering me a sip of her Smart Water. "Your type has sort of turned out to be your enemy."

Marina and I roamed around in our conversation from books to politics to monologues to men, jabbering at each other incessantly in bars, cafés, parks, apartments, the subway, and once at a Denny's midway between San Francisco and L.A. where Marina ordered, rather memorably, a side order of peas for dinner. We goofed about with tarot cards—I generally got the one symbolizing death and pestilence—and made one another laugh over self-help books like *How to Find Your Soul Mate in One Year or Less.*

Pray!

Blind yourself with pokers!

We glowered when we read the Sunday *New York Times* and came across the arguments of conservative Washington women who hissed that we only had ourselves to blame for being childless, because (so they suspected) we selfishly whooped it up in our twenties and broke the hearts of decent men, until—*ha!*—there were no decent men left, the train had pulled out of the station, and we were still on the platform with our hangovers and packets of condoms.

"What is it with these women?" Marina would ask me, wide-eyed. "As if the little tin-pot dictators they call husbands, who run around the Beltway doing punditry with spittle at the corners of their sneers, are some sort of shining example of masculine decency."

Believe me, I would happily have settled down if I

could have. But I could not. I always got into the same galling quandary. The men I fell for were handsome to the point of being spoiled. They had no sense of scarcity in love and would not rest content. Maybe I was fabulous and then again maybe someone more fabulous was just then sauntering down Fifth Avenue. It was a doomed model for a woman seeking to make something of a bright, constructive love. So I just carried on with the parts of my life that I had some control over, like my work and . . . well, that's about it.

"Your love map takes you in circles," Marina said, dabbing at her mouth with a napkin.

She was referring to a book my mother once sent me after she felt particularly perturbed by the manner in which one of my boyfriends had bolted. My mother was a psychologist, who generally communicated with me by sending psychoanalytic texts by parcel post. *Love Maps* came accompanied by a typically perfunctory note. "Re: Charles, not exact, but interesting if extrapolated." The book was by a "sexologist" named John Money, who studies sexual deviants such as pedophiles and necrophiles in order to understand how they come to have such grossly inappropriate types.

"Look, I'm sorry, Jack, you're a great guy but you're just not my thing. I like men with glassy, staring eyes and rigor mortis."

"*Why?*"

"Don't ask me why, Jack. The heart wants what it wants."

For Money, our hearts followed a map that was imprinted on us in childhood, unconsciously and by chance. Some people were destined to fall in love with corpses and others with Charles. "I like to think about it in terms of your very first crush," Marina said, gingerly removing a grain of brown rice from her tooth. She had flipped through *Love Maps* in my office. "I'm pretty sure that's where we start going wrong, right off the bat. I went nuts for George Michael, who was the first of how many who turned out to be gay? And that was because my father was gay, even if he wasn't out of the closet then, I somehow picked it up. So who did you fall for?"

I thought about it. "Captain Haddock in the Tin-Tin comics."

Tin-Tin was a Belgian boy hero, plucky and spindly, who kept rescuing people and solving jewel heists with his little dog, Snowy. Captain Haddock was his friend, who was constantly soused on whiskey. "Blistering blue barnacles!" Captain Haddock would drunkenly thunder, as he charged around in his fisherman's turtleneck, sporting a jaunty seaman's cap. He was always in a temper. His shoulders were broad, his beard was dark, and his masculinity was reckless and forceful.

Alas, as often happens at that age, my crush went unrequited. To my knowledge, only my Aunt Bea ever managed to meet the object of her girlish romantic obsession, and that was pure bloody-mindedness on her part. She fell in love with the actor Roddy McDowall after seeing him in *How Green Was My Valley* when she was thirteen, at which point she banged her head repeatedly against the sidewalk cement in a genteel suburb of Arlington,

Virginia, until her greatly perturbed father agreed to invite McDowall to a cocktail party. Since he was the Canadian ambassador to Washington at the time, he managed to pull it off, and Aunt Bea was rewarded for her head wound with the glancing touch of Roddy McDowell's hand as he wended his way through the receiving line.

In any event, when I think about it now, what Captain Haddock sparked in my heart was not so much a yearning for men who were tall, drunk, and handsome, as a decided predilection for cartoon characters. I dated men who lacked depth and maturity, and I was able to do so by projecting a suitable personality entirely of my own devising onto their monosyllabic selves. Women are very artful at this because of the amount of time they spend as little girls playing with their dolls. I know that doll play is all about young females rehearsing their destiny to be tender and nurturing mothers. But the other skill we develop in this exercise is the ability to take a chunk of molded plastic and assign it an extremely elaborate emotional life conveniently entwined with our own.

Consider Bob, the weight lifter. I surrendered my virginity to him when I was sixteen. He held dumbbells aloft in the basement of our high school, surfacing only to eat and sit stiffly through classes. Those are the facts, to which I can add absolutely nothing that doesn't come from my imagination. "Dear Bob," I once wrote to him, in a masterful act of projection, "I've never gotten into weight lifting and you certainly take no notice of literature or the theater, and we never talk the way I do with my friends, because you don't like listening to my problems, but you're still so essential to me. I need your caring to care about what I do."

According to my diary, I broke up with him two months later, after proposing, with all the melodramatic flair of a typical seventeen-year-old, that he had to choose between me or weight lifting. It was a no-brainer.

All the men I dated after that would leave me, sooner or later, without articulating a coherent reason, because there never was one, just a vague sense of missed opportunity, of other women still Out There.

Charles, the inspiration for Mom sending me *Love Maps*, broke up with me in a restaurant during his lunch hour. In exchange for the year we had lived together he gave me forty-five minutes in a crowded public place and informed me, by way of prelude, that I had some really fine qualities. It was like getting fired.

"Please don't take it personally," he advised while I dissolved in my soup bowl. "You'll make somebody a wonderful wife and mother some day."

This was not the sort of information I found helpful. Somewhere along the great divide of our little café table, amidst the small but growing pile of shredded napkin on my side and the merrily diminishing cheeseburger on his, my distress signals failed to get through.

"I can't believe this!" I finally burst out, drawing a reproachful stare from the waiter. "You don't want to talk about it, you're just going to let the whole relationship go?"

"Well, I won't let it go," he replied, smiling, with an

oh-silly-Frannie expression on his face. "I'll always be your friend. You can always call me up." He lent me enough money for a cab.

Marina, then at acting school, and my friend Ellie, who worked at the Canadian Consulate, bought Sobrani cigarettes and Absolut and settled in, cross-legged for the tale. At times like this we were kids in a tree fort. We traded our ex-lovers' parting lines like baseball cards. Whose was most banal? Most incongruous? Most entirely beside the point of our heartbreak? We didn't always remember what we said, distracted as we were by the sound of the sky falling, but we all agreed we heard a cheerful, distant voice in the din. Someone chatting on the radio? No, the Men We Love. We assured ourselves that the ones who left weren't intending to be so cavalier. They were acting on impulse, they hadn't worked it out yet. And if they had, they concealed their motives, so all there was left was consolation or a change of subject. Utterances to fill poignant, stretching silences with sound.

I learned nothing except to suspect myself. I spun Charles's exit phrases around in my head for weeks—examining them every which way, excavating the site of my romance, hunting for relics of meaning. I tried, for instance, to puzzle out the statements "don't take it personally," and "it isn't you, it's me." It went on all day, every day, like having a song stuck in my head to which I didn't know the words. What can he mean that it isn't me? He isn't leaving anybody else. I tried to spell the logic out, see if it made any sense. It's not you that I'm not in love with, it's me who is not in love with you.

Was that what he meant? And if so, what did he mean?

The line about my really fine qualities became an endless source of empty torment. Was it only women with really poor qualities who held on to intimacy? Women who were bitchy, aloof, eternally and temptingly uncertain about love? I thought about ways I could downplay my qualities. I thought about phoning Charles. "Uh, about my qualities—can you be more specific about which ones work, which ones don't?" I studied women in the movies. Conducted an informal survey. Which ones had their romances fall apart for intangible reasons? It was not a popular plot device.

Two years later, when I fell in love again on a summer trip home to Toronto, the phrase *soul mate* even flashed through my mind. He was funny and sexy and graceful and bold. He teased me until I blushed. We constructed a private dialogue of intimacies like twins with their secret language. We laid down our confidences as a foundation, built intricate passageways and codes, hand signals, and winks of the eye. But all it took was a kick from his running-shoed foot and our sandcastle future fell apart.

It happened on a rooftop on a humid August evening. His cousin from Europe was visiting just then and she waited, bewildered, to be given some dinner while I experienced déjà vu over her head. He didn't want a girlfriend, he told me, his gorgeous features inscrutable in the twilight. He wanted more time to just concentrate on his work. And yes, here we go again. "It's not you, Frannie . . ."

Could his body have been possessed by the spirit of

my former boyfriend? Is that really you talking? You talking to me? "I don't regret the time we spent together," I heard him consoling as I lit the wrong end of my cigarette and dropped the rest of my matches in a tar-slick rain puddle. "You were an important part of my life."

Were. He asked me if I wanted to stick around for dinner, maybe some pizza with him and his cousin. I declined. He lent me enough money for a cab to the airport.

I gathered up his lines with my weekend bag and sought out my friends in the tree fort. It still helped to make light of our common experience. But as we headed past thirty, the comic relief grew a little less comforting. We dreaded the thought that this was all we were working with: pickup lines and parting lines, like two neat parentheses around incidental excursions into love.

The sky had clouded over and a misting rain began to fall. Marina and I headed back to the office, bumping against one another companionably as we walked. I wanted to tell her about the pregnancy—her, of all people—but I remained almost helplessly silent.

"Don't worry about Calvin," she said. "Just enjoy his company. It's better that you're not head over heels, in a way, because you can take it one step at a time."

Some Thoughts on Being a Mess

I am not a neat woman. I share this ineptitude with my father, who is so puzzled by domestic chores that he would rather be stuck in an elevator with bees than pit his fragile confidence against an unwaxed floor. My mother and my siblings tidy hungrily and obsessively, as if they can straighten out the meaning of their lives with Mr. Clean. I am their opposite. When my life gets confusing I fall into complete disarray.

When I break up with men, I tend to lose my wallet in taxis and phone booths, or forget my coat in restaurants. When I fight with my mother, I leave the tap running in the bathroom. Once, when I got laid off from a job that I loved, I locked myself out of my apartment two times in a week and fell down a manhole.

My mother calls it "being in a state."

"For heaven's sake, Frances, you're in a state," she'll

say, in a tone that is at once dismissive, irritable, and knowing. She tells all of her friends about it, I'm fairly certain, offering the latest exasperated anecdote about her youngest daughter, whom she has airily declared to be the sole resident of the state of plight. I try not to think about these condescending conversations far away.

My mother's crowd recalls, however, that I developed an anxiety disorder in my early twenties, after a prolonged period of reckless living and emotional mishaps that culminated in an alarming episode in which I grew frightened of my own feet. I was standing in my mother's kitchen, about to take my first anti-anxiety tablet, when I looked down and realized with a gasp that I didn't recognize my feet. In their stead, I saw pale rectangular objects with jutting appendages splayed flat against the floor tiles. What were feet, if not as lunatic an arrangement of flesh as a one-eyed alien? Oh God, I panicked, these . . . these feet things are not Of Me.

According to my mother, I was having an Existential Anxiety Attack, which is stage four in the progress of the disorder from Valid Anxiety to Irrational Anxiety to Paralytic Anxiety About Everything, Constantly to the grand finale of feeling dissociated from one's feet. It is difficult to remember to clean the oven in circumstances such as these.

Granted, ten years later that shouldn't still be my excuse, but today, Miss Frances Mackenzie, sole resident of the state of plight, has been attempting all morning to wrap her head around the implications of unplanned motherhood, and has, as a result, affixed her palm to the refrigerator with super-adhesive wood glue.

"What are you doing with wood glue?" Marina asked, after I'd finally reached her on the phone, about an hour after noticing that I was tethered to a large appliance.

"It was in my drawer; I think Calvin was using it. I wanted to fix the heel on my shoe," I explained. "I spilled it on my hand, and I mean, you gotta think the warning should be a little more explicit on these tubes. This is not the time for fine print. This is the time for very large print. Maybe even an audible warning system."

Marina arrived half an hour later with some solvent and a soy Frappucino. "This is the trouble with you, Frannie," she observed, seamlessly resuming our conversation from the previous week. "You attract your type like flies—"

"Yes I do, because I'm covered in fucking glue."

"But listen to me, but you can't hold on to them because when all is said and done, brawny boys want mommies. They want women who'll take care of them, and draw the line when they're being jerks, and make them change their underwear. You know? And you're a lovely woman, but you're kind of off-duty in the domestic sphere. Which is fine," she added, overriding my stammered objections, "but not for that type of man. That type of guy needs an anchor, and you're a sail."

"What kind of metaphor is that?"

"But you know what I mean. Come on. You can't even keep your apartment at a rudimentary level of hygiene."

"Why should I?" I protested defensively. "Nobody important comes here."

I knew she was right. It's a decided disadvantage, being messy when you're female. Women aren't supposed to be slobs, even if they're fantastically ambitious, even if they're Tina Brown or Diane Sawyer. Women are supposed to be neat freaks and fashion mavens, sleek as kittens and scented like heaven. It is both incomprehensible and disturbing to see a woman in mismatched socks.

A monstrous double standard, I've always felt. When I was in college, the dormitory maids kept tattling on me to the dean of women for leaving apple cores and empty wine bottles strewn about my room. But the men, who managed to erect amazing infrastructures out of pizza boxes, beer cans, and underpants, so that the maids had to crawl through tunnels of litter just to enter their rooms, were apparently being lovable. Oh, those boys.

Boys will be boys, and women should not be freaks.

I remember watching Barbara Walters's TV tête-à-tête with Monica Lewinsky—how Walters oozed sycophancy as Lewinsky confessed to fellatio under desks, adultery with a president, lying her head off, having an abortion, being doped up on Prozac—a truly sordid array of behaviors.

But Walters only became thoroughly and alertly probing on the subject of the semen-stained dress. Why did Lewinsky not *dry clean* it? Was it a tawdry souvenir? A weapon of blackmail? No, the poor girl protested, she honestly just bunched it up and threw it in her closet because that's what she did with her clothes.

Walters was astonished. I was like, yeah, I get that, totally.

"I'm a mess," I'd confessed apologetically to Calvin when he first saw my apartment.

"Maybe so," he replied, "but you're a fine mess."

What's not to love about a man who says that, I wondered now, as I rubbed my hand contemplatively with glue solvent.

Yogi Naryana:
Tell Me What to Do!

Lately, I've been thinking about destiny. For instance, what is it? An actual phenomenon? Or a curse muttered under the breath? Why would it be my destiny to be an impoverished single mother who will never again stay up past midnight drinking cosmopolitans at Temple Bar, whereas Madonna has no such destiny?

Surely it could not be my destiny to give birth to a child and then leave her on the steps of an orphanage, as if I were living in rural New England before the war. That's an insensible destiny. I couldn't possibly think of a plausible excuse for surrendering a child to adoption at my age. But then what is my fate instead? Am I destined to return to Canada, where I have free health insurance but no job? Or is my destiny to win $10 million in a lottery, and move to a villa in Mexico, where I can hire a twenty-four-hour nanny and shout out "leaf!" to the gardener every time one falls in the pool?

I wonder if I was truly destined to slog it out with Calvin? Is that why I got pregnant before I could correctly spell his last name? Why am I not destined to swan slenderly through London soirees on the arms of Francesco What's-his-face, that gorgeous Italian gazillionaire I met in Paris the summer that I was nineteen? He was smart, he was funny, he adored me, and I—being a stupid idiot—balked, because he wasn't Captain Haddock.

All this weighed very much on my mind, but I found no consoling certainties in the platitudes of my culture. I had no priest to confess to, no shrink who could nudge me along, no village elder to banish me to the farthest hut. Marina, when I broke the news, was a supportive champion of Whatever I Wanted to Do. Which was what? There wasn't any consensus. I floated through space. I walked across a bridge without handrails.

I consulted a psychic, at one of those expos out at the Jacob Javits Center. She offered that I was allergic to cheese.

"How about this?" Marina asked, showing me a book that had been delivered to the reception desk for review. She read out the title: *The Secret Language of Destiny: A Personology Guide to Finding Your Life Purpose.* I took it from her and scanned the back. The jacket pegged it "as the ultimate sourcebook for answering one of life's great questions."

"Another one of life's questions," Marina observed, "is what the hell is personology?"

We looked it up in the dictionary, to no avail. *Personol-*

ogy was a baldly made-up word. This gave me a fleeting idea. Maybe I could finance motherhood by concocting my own -ology for the self-help market, based on an intricate formulation of absolute truth and certain wisdoms understood exclusively by me. I could call it Frannie-ology. Why not? One of the principal tenets of the Fran-ological worldview will be that destiny cannot be found in a coffee-table book.

I know this to be true, because I read *The Secret Language of Destiny* in the Temple Bar that night while glumly nursing a cranberry juice and soda, and discovered, based on my birth date, that my destiny is to be on the "karmic path of tenderness"—a destiny so vague that I could either join the Sisters of Mercy in Calcutta or get scalded by a boiler, and both would suit my personological fate.

"Those on the Way of Tenderness," the book proclaimed, "are here to release their need to be in control and to go in search of their inner sensitivity." Therefore I was destined to have a baby, because pregnancy makes me . . . well . . . sensitive is an understatement. When I'm in Calvin's apartment and he goes to the bathroom, I feel rejected and burst into tears.

Voilà. My karmic destiny is to be pregnant. I share this destiny, according to the book, with Joan Crawford, Carly Simon, and Lou Costello.

"Don't cry, Frannie," Calvin pleaded, standing in the doorway of his flat. His old leather jacket was damp with rain, and his hair stuck in clumps to his forehead. He eased a six pack of Samuel Adams beer out of a wet paper bag and regarded me warily as I lay on my back on his futon, my trembling fingers chasing the tears which slid crookedly across my face. My breath came in hiccuping gulps. A small television flickered in the corner of the room, in between a gleaming pile of unassembled motorcycle parts, and Calvin's prized Brazilian cherry-wood marimba. He put the beer down on his bookshelf.

"Are you crying because I went to the store?"

"Noooo!" I sobbed, flailing my arm in his general direction as if to swat at the suggestion.

"Do you want to talk about it?"

"No."

He slipped off his coat, waiting.

"It's just this commercial I saw on television."

He walked over and sat on the futon. "You're crying about a TV commercial?"

"I can't explain it," I sobbed. "It was an ad for All State Insurance, where the guy's holding his baby daughter and then the baby becomes a school girl and then she's graduating from college and they go all the way through to her wedding and it's just like a *whole life*, you know?"

Calvin lay carefully down beside me and cupped his chin in his hand. "And your point is . . . ?"

"Oh, fuck off." I swept away my tears in irritation, as if the curtain had to close on the show because the audience was all wrong. He caught at my wrist and kissed my hand.

"I don't think I knew how sensitive you were when I first met you," he murmured, studying my face.

"I'm not sensitive!" I protested.

"Well, you kind of are, Frannie. I mean, I'm sorry to point this out, but you've burst into tears twice now in bars because of the tunes they were playing, one of which was an absolutely dreadful cover of a Peter, Paul and Mary song that was cloying to begin with. And you cried when you discovered a long line at the bank on Friday, and that other time we went to the deli, and they'd run out of Rice Krispies squares. You cried."

He smoothed my fine, flyaway hair from my forehead. "And now you're crying about an insurance ad." He paused, as if the ludicrousness of my behavior was hovering at the edge of his consciousness, eluding his grasp. Instead, he gave it a romantic spin. "I've never met a woman with such an intriguing mix of cynicism and sentimentality," he said.

"I'm not sentimental!" I argued, without much authority under the circumstances. I felt a flash of contempt for him, for actually chalking this up to my normal state of being. I rolled away to face the wall and sighed deeply. I couldn't decide which was worse at this point: confessing that I was going to have his baby, or letting him carry on thinking that I was a cute, weepy little fool who wouldn't let him out of my sight. It was humiliating.

Why he took it in stride, I did not know. I wondered if it was because his last girlfriend was such a cold, withholding strumpet. Stupid and beady-eyed, and unable to make up her mind until he told her to blow it out her flute. I hated her ferociously, never having met her.

Perhaps he liked being clung to and adored for a

change. But he'd tire of the simpering. And I couldn't stop, because I'd never felt so vulnerable in my life. I began to cry again.

"Look, Frannie, I don't know why I'm making you so insecure," he ventured.

—oh for God's sake—

"But you shouldn't be, because you're the most amazing person I've ever met." He said this in a whisper, pressing his face into my shoulder.

(Why do we think there's less at stake for men when they declare themselves this way?) I lay still, as if holding my breath. No more please, not yet. But I felt the reassurance like a warming sip of whiskey.

"I don't want you to worry when I'm in Europe," he added, "because all I'll be doing is thinking about you." He sang a snatch of Neil Young in a rough, self-conscious murmur: "like a coin that won't get tossed, rolling home to you."

I closed my eyes, and found myself adrift in a tranquil ocean, where gratitude, grief, fear, and love flowed together as inseparable currents.

"I want you to have a good time in Europe, Calvin," I eventually managed to say. "I promise I'm not going to stagger around New York bawling my head off." I stretched my arm out and clasped his hand. "Please don't worry about me. Really."

I thought I might take a trip, myself, while he was gone. A trip home was the notion that compelled me. I just didn't know for certain where home was.

The Apple of My Eye

When one lives in New York, all other cities are insubstantial by comparison; no matter how fine they are, how lively and aspiring, they invariably become small, plodding, too-eager burgs in the eyes of the young they've so carefully tended, who've fled them. Where am I, one asks, upon disembarking from an airplane that lifted off at La Guardia. Not New York? Why, then I must be above the treeline! Help, help!

Having lived in Manhattan for nine years, I was, like most New Yorkers, in the habit of darting in and out of other places with anxious swiftness, as if afraid to stay too long and perish from ennui. Thus I leaped into the back of a cab at Pearson International Airport in Toronto and barked at the driver: downtown, northwest corner of College and Yonge. *Vite, vite.* No point going to Mum's first. All I had with me was a shoulder bag. I'd do this free medical checkup, stay the weekend, and then off. I had promised The Editor I'd be back on Tuesday, to edit the Annie Dillard essay on pond life and the meaning of God.

"Do you come from Toronto?" the cabdriver asked. He was a good-looking man, dark and fine-featured, with relaxed, intelligent eyes. He was wearing a baseball cap and a pair of earmuffs, with a plaid scarf wound around his neck. It wasn't that cold.

"I suppose I'm from Toronto. I live in New York, now."

"Aha! New York!" He gave out a deep bark of a laugh. "I lived in New York also. When I first came to North America. I drove a taxi there." He smiled into his rearview.

"Well, that must have been hellish," I said, returning his smile.

He laughed again. "Listen to me, it was like a bad dream, like the dream you have of being in front of the classroom, or on the stage." He spoke fluent English, but it was oddly inflected, an English vocabulary with a Franco-African rhythm, so that I had to lean forward to catch what he said.

"Where did you come from?" I asked.

"Burundi. The Congo. I was a doctor."

"How did you wind up in Toronto?"

"Oh, by accident. Some friends asked me to come up with them from New York in a car. For a holiday. I thought we were going to Montreal. I had never heard of Toronto. Only Montreal. I thought Quebec was the capital of Canada. We crossed at Buffalo, but then I couldn't get back into America. I didn't have the right papers. *Alors, je suis resté ici.* Do you speak French?"

"*Un peu*," I offered, noncommittally. I took it for years and years, of course. *Je suis, tu est, il est. Où est le bar?* Not much use for it in Manhattan. We gunned it down the 427 along the city's western flank, in a race for our lives with thousands of other cars all hurtling along at 80 mph for no particular reason. The only place more frightening to drive is Texas, in my experience, but that is because Texans are macho, whereas Torontonians are repressed, and can only ever express their competitive rage on the road.

I stared out the window at the slate-gray expanse of Lake Ontario. Every time I came home, there were more and more glass condominium towers steepling upward along its shore, being bought up, my mother said, by wealthy gentlemen from Iran and Hong Kong who were hastily transferring their money from less congenial homelands.

Toronto is a city filled with accidental citizens. They come from everywhere, from Argentina, Nigeria, Russia, Pakistan, but rarely because they have an explicit vision of the place; they aren't drawn by mythic images of riches and glamor like the immigrants arriving at the airports and harbors of New York. They are exiles, for the most part, who have thrown darts at a map of the world. Arriving, astonished by the cold, bewildered by hockey and our Nordic reserve, they nonetheless build their cities within our city: Chinatown, Little India, Portugal Town. Our city becomes a new city surprised by itself, doubletaking at the profusion of culture: Brazilian dance clubs, Indian cricket matches, Polish delis, Chinese newspapers, Ecuadorian snack stands, somber Italian Easter parades.

It's wonderfully spiced, this city, but there's no point arguing that in the corridors of *The Pithy Review.* Toronto is Canada. Canada? Bland. Clean. Nice. Boring. Polite. Lots of weather. Weather and hockey players. Not much else up there. "Canada has, what, four million people?" a friend of mine at *The New York Times* once asked me. "No, about thirty million." So, what's the difference? None of them are Madonna. Blandnicecleanboringpolite. Lots of weather. Cold up there, huh?

My loyalties were awkwardly divided. I was besotted with New York. I felt like a courtier at Versailles who periodically toured the provinces to take the air and find myself encircled by the curious: What news of the king? I walked among my countrymen with a cloak of unimpeachable authority, possessing greater enlightenment, effortless superiority, being a Sneetch with a star etched upon my belly.

On the other hand, what's bred in the bone, as Robertson Davies pointed out. He was a novelist. Canadian.

For God's Sake,
Stop Drinking Espressos

"Frances Mackenzie?"

Doctor Nandha poked her head out of the examining room and peered around the waiting area. I trotted dutifully toward her, folding up my newspaper and stuffing it into my shoulder bag.

"Frances, how are you?" she asked, without even the slightest flicker of curiosity, bending her head to my chart.

"All right."

"So you're here for a pregnancy exam."

"Yes."

"Have you had a test?"

"No, but I've been vomiting into sweaters."

She nodded. My kingdom for a medical professional who acknowledges a joke.

"Well, we can tell easily enough with an internal." She

pushed her shining dark hair behind her ears and slapped on a pair of latex gloves, encouraging me to disrobe, don a sheet, lie down, and spread my legs louchely on her white-papered examining table.

"This will feel cold," she warned, before stuffing what appeared to be a stapler up my vaginal canal. I heard the metal make a screwing sound and just wished that she'd *cut it out. Right now.*

"Your cervix is certainly tinged blue," she murmured. "That's a definite sign."

Before I had time to pummel her with my fists she removed the stapler, which squelched, and then prodded my abdomen impassively. As an afterthought, she palpated my breasts, which provoked shrieking.

"Okay, you can get dressed, Frances. You're almost certainly pregnant. Do you remember when you last had your period?"

"No."

"Well, we can date it with an ultrasound. Are you planning to go through with the pregnancy?"

"Yeah, I think so." Since she asked, I was overwhelmed with the desire to burst into a monologue about choices and destinies and maternal mystery and the nature of love and— never mind. She had turned her back curtly and was scribbling on a pad.

"I assume you've stopped drinking alcohol, and you'll need to cut out coffee and nicotine and any drugs. If you have a headache, you can take Advil. Anything else, I'd like you to consult me first, all right?"

She handed me a pamphlet about what to eat—mostly

broccoli, fish, wheat toast, mangos, fifteen servings of protein, twelve of dairy, whole bison, suckling pigs, everything else available in the supermarket, daily—and slipped out of the room.

Across the street from Bedford Medical Associates was a Starbucks, perkily inhabiting the high-vaulted interior of an old, austere Bank of Montreal building. I poked my head in curiously, and decided to stand in line for a treat. Exhorting myself to be conscientious about the food I was eating, I contemplated the egg salad pita wrap. Why put egg salad in a pita? All it does is explode out one end when you bite into the other, like a bizarre little boiled egg jack-in-the-box. Does pita give people a satisfying hint of the Middle East while catering to their baser desire to eat North American comfort food? Should we bake tuna casserole in phyllo pastry? Make baklava with marshmallows? That might be good, actually.

I was thinking about this, and wondering if I had enough change in my pocket at any rate, when suddenly I heard a familiar voice. It was a calm, amused contralto: "Frannie Mackenzie . . ."

I swung around in surprise. "Ellie!" She had a half-smile playing on her lips, and crinkle lines—more pronounced now—spidering out from the corners of her hazel eyes, as if the mere sight of me inspired the prospect of hilarity. It was arguably a smirk, but that was an argument I had loyally countered when Ellie was my flatmate in SoHo and my boyfriends of the time remarked suspiciously upon her manner. They sensed her capacity to damn them, which she did. There was a yen for stern judgment lurking beneath Ellie's good-humored calm. I always thought of it as defensive. If my boyfriends left me, Fed Exing their lies about "space," I was consoled by the rallying intimacy of my female friendships. Ellie damned men for leaving me in advance.

"Hey Ellie!" I leaned forward to embrace her. Her hair smelled like apples. She had woven it into two plaits, which I'd never seen on her before. Her outfit was markedly different, as well. Not a whiff of Betsey Johnson in her denim overalls, underneath which she was wearing a stone-gray turtleneck sweater. Functional. She looked functional, which was new for Ellie. She used to look like she'd just crawled out of a haystack with a farm boy and hadn't yet pulled down her skirt.

"It's lovely to see you," I said. She spread out her arms and gave a little shrug, as if to say "who knew I was here?"

"How long has it been?"

We had pulled away from each other after she'd married Gavin with a spectacularly expensive wedding in the Puck Building on Houston Street. Gavin was a bellicose sports reporter. He berated people, especially Ellie, for insignificant transgressions, such as daring to disagree with him about whether Vince Carter was a better basketball player than Magic Henderson. I could barely talk to Gavin because I didn't know anything about sports and he took that as a sign of rank stupidity.

Ellie seemed to rise to these arguments, however, with

an unexpected fervor, matching him blow for blow. She parried him and she also mothered him, taking satisfaction in his rescue—in being the one woman who saw through his bluster and recognized the needy infant within. From my vantage point, seeing through Gavin held as much fulfillment as seeing through a fat man's shorts when he bends over: Behold! An asshole.

"What are you doing here?" Ellie asked, fishing her wallet out of a large canvas bag to suggest that we should resume standing in line.

"I'm just visiting my parents, and then I was just . . . near here, and I wanted a coffee."

"Well, do you have a minute to sit down?"

"Absolutely."

I ordered the egg salad pita wrap and an espresso. Ellie ordered herbal tea. "I'm still breastfeeding Lucas," she explained as we scraped back our hard, straight chairs and sat down.

"Lucas, oh my God!" I cried. "I haven't even met him yet, he must be two years old!"

"He'll be two next month. I have a picture." She rummaged around and pulled out a snapshot of a green-eyed baby peering out of a pot on the stove. His pink mouth formed a perfect square, like he was halfway between smiling and wailing. "Gavin put him there," Ellie chuckled.

"He's beautiful," I murmured. I was mesmerized by the mingling of Gavin and Ellie in this tiny child. I got to wondering about me and Calvin, and whether it wouldn't be fun to take two of our baby pictures and play around with them in PhotoShop. Then I involuntarily clutched my face in terror, the way I was tending to these days, whenever the reality of my condition suddenly shot up my spine. I glanced down at my coffee, which was almost gone. I wanted another.

"So, you don't even have caffeine while you're breast-feeding?" I asked her.

"Oh God, no." She shook her head adamantly and smiled. "I haven't touched alcohol or caffeine in nearly three years. They say one drink on the day of conception can lower your baby's IQ." I did a rough mental calculation.

"I'm dying for a cocktail," Ellie confided. "What I wouldn't give, even, for a spritzer, you know? Just something even that tame." She gazed wistfully out the window and fiddled with her braid. "I don't even eat anything with food coloring or artificial flavor. Lucas eats organic everything. It costs more, but . . ." She shrugged.

I decided that either I was in trouble, or she was insane.

"But not even coffee?" I wondered. "What could happen?"

"I just don't want to risk it," she answered, which wasn't really an answer, I felt. Look at Shakespeare. His mother probably drank nothing but flagons of mead and he did pretty well. What about—I don't know—Jean-Paul Sartre! Obstetricians in Paris insisted that pregnant women drink red wine every day "for the iron." And look at him: He came up with *Being and Nothingness*. Hell, what of the Irish? Their entire nourishment from birth to death was boiled bloody potatoes. They probably didn't have much use for pregnancy diet books. What would the authors say? "It may be tempting to reach for that potato, but just remember, baby eats what you eat! Try to limit yourself to half a potato on special occasions, or better yet, go without. Nine months for you is a lifetime for your child. Air may taste blander, but baby will thank you."

I wanted another coffee desperately. I went back to the counter to order a latte. Better than an espresso, no? I could split the nutritional difference fifty-fifty with the baby. Milk for you and drugs for me.

I put off telling Ellie I was pregnant.

At My Age

"You're going to have to acknowledge this pregnancy sooner or later," my mother said. She was tidying up in the kitchen when I got home after coffee with Ellie. Sunlight slanted in from the back garden and washed faintly over the white vinyl tiles of the floor, the toaster, the kettle, the burbling radio. I sat despondently on a bar stool at her faded yellow Formica counter, examining a jar of lemon curd. It's amazing how mothers manage to keep you young. If you could only translate the mother-daughter dynamic into a recipe for anti-wrinkle cream, you could stuff it into a bottle and thereafter look no older than fourteen.

"What are you talking about?" I asked, looking up at her warily. She was a tall woman, my mother, with impeccable posture, as if she'd spent the better part of her life wearing a neck ruff, instead of the invariable off-white woolen turtleneck paired with "slacks." (We abandoned slacks as a noun, haven't we, and I can't think why.)

"Dr. Nandha's office didn't phone to book an obstetrical ultrasound for *me*," she replied, arching one brow.

The blood rushed to my cheeks. I shifted the subject without dropping it. "I suppose you're going to leave a psychoanalytic text on my pillow again."

She frowned, taking an extra swipe at her counter. "Well, when did I do that?"

"When I was twenty, and you caught me spending the night with Charlie in a hotel after I told you I was staying at Sarah Graham's cottage. You left *The Psychology of Lying* on my pillow."

"Ah," she laughed. "That was a remarkable bit of dissembling on your part. You even gave me a vivid description of the gnats and mosquitoes, and how you didn't have enough insect repellant. Imagine my confusion when you rang off and I bumped into Sarah at the supermarket."

"Well, if you hadn't stuck me in boarding school, we would have talked about s-e-x by then and I wouldn't have felt so uncomfortable letting you know where I was."

She slapped her dishtowel lightly against the faucet and lifted her kettle onto the burner to make herself a glass of Neo Citron. I sighed. She turned to face me, folding her arms across her chest and eyeing me curiously. "Is this good news or bad news?" she asked. She still spoke with her Edinburgh accent, even though she'd

been living in Toronto for forty years. I busied myself trying to remove a jam stain from the counter with my fin-
gernail.

"Suffice it to say," I allowed, "that you're going to have
another grandchild."

My sister, Annabelle, provided the first five, and was
now buried under the rubble somewhere in the British
Columbia interior. She got pregnant so easily that the
happy announcements began to embarrass her, as if her
fecundity had grown unseemly. She grew loathe to
broadcast the news, gritting her teeth and muttering
something wryly sarcastic to my mother in postcards
from Whistler. In my case, the news was accompanied by
an importunate need to vomit. I clenched my jaw.

She considered me silently for a moment, and then her
face lit up and she emitted an odd little squeak. "Eeep!
That's marvelous!" She scurried around to my side of the
counter and squeezed me in a hug.

"When are you due?"

"I don't know, early winter."

"Can I tell your father?"

"Oh God, please don't."

She veritably skipped over to her kettle, and then suddenly stood still and regarded me in puzzlement. "Who's
the father?"

"Ah," I said, canting my head and chewing on my
thumbnail, "well, he's Canadian. And his name is Calvin.
And he's from Cape Breton." I paused. "That's all I know."

"Oh for heaven's sake," my mother said, looking decidedly put out.

"Mum, I'm exaggerating, I know more than that. I just haven't been involved with him for very long. He's very, very nice, don't worry."

"Well, so what's his name?"

"Calvin Puddie. Spelled P-u-d-d-i-e." I'd finally sorted that out, and felt newly authoritative. "It's Acadian. I suppose it was pronounced differently in the original French."

She had obviously never heard of the name and her mouth worked soundlessly for a moment. "What does his father do?"

"He was a coal miner."

She picked up her dish towel and started polishing the counter again, trying to imagine her new relations. "My grandchild will be descended from a long line of coal-mining Puddies."

I glared at her. "That's one way to characterize it. Your grandchild will also have antlers, because I drank an obscene number of cocktails before I realized I was pregnant."

"Oh, don't worry too much about that," she muttered, as if wearying, suddenly, of the conversation. "We all drank highballs before dinner and it didn't do any of you much harm."

She had more pressing concerns, and you could see them press at her temples as she took the kettle off the stove and sat down heavily at the kitchen table.

"You're not upset by this, are you, Mum?" I asked. "Because if you're upset, then I'll get upset, and I can't really afford to be upset under the circumstances. I have to just—"

She interrupted me. "There is nothing inherently upsetting about a woman in her thirties having a child, Frances. You are a member of what must be the first generation of women in history who continue to perceive themselves as teenaged mothers fifteen years past high school."

She tilted her head and tugged at the neck of her turtleneck. "I am certainly not upset."

I waited for a moment and then, since she evidently had nothing to add, I slid off my stool and headed upstairs. I had no desire at all to field further queries. I just wanted to lie down, torment myself for a while, and have a nap.

A Lesson in Self-torment

Torment yourself over your inability to confess. Accuse your-self of being a coward.

"You were born anxious," my mother likes to say. That gets her rather conveniently off the hook. But I do re-member having numerous abiding terrors as a child. One was that I would perish in an Ice Age. I would be an adult, living somewhere green and sweet-smelling, and all of a sudden the glaciers at the North Pole would begin a silent southward march. With gathering speed, towers of ice as wide as cities would surge across the treeline, crushing hills and flattening houses. They would trap me like an insect in amber, with my mouth caught for eter-nity in a round, surprised O.

I remember learning about the Ice Age in school. We traced the Time-Life book chart of the earth's history, this era and that, layered like parfait. We color-photocopied pages with our crayons, shading the vast, unfathomable passage of history with pretty Crayola hues. I must not have understood eras and ages, because I couldn't see how there could be more years than the years in my life, and that it would take more years than that for the great polar ice sheets to spread. Or maybe I did understand that, but thought, as I often did as a child, that the facts were unreliable. My elder sister Annabelle agreed with me. The earth could spin off its axis, why not? she argued to my mother. Laws could change. There might be a new, speedier sort of Ice Age, we concurred. With this way of thinking, I managed to be afraid of pretty much bloody everything, from the prospect at age five that mice would steal my dresses to the certainty at age sixteen that my best friend was French-kissing Bob.

On the other hand, there were many fearful things I did not fear. It never occurred to me that there was danger in jumping off the green-shingled roof of our garage in a deliberate attempt to break my leg. I saw the end results of falls and jumps among my friends: a cast that everyone at school would sign. That was worthy of pursuit. Nor did I see risk in playing a game called Ghost with my brother David, wherein I would stand giggling in the cellar while David, in his role as the poltergeist, knelt on the kitchen above me and slid a steak knife through a hole in the floor. More than once it fell and clattered at my feet and, by sheer coincidence, did not stab me through the head.

I had a mad, complacent trust in the world I moved through. But for my imagined fate I never dreamed sweetly, only of peril.

"The basis of optimism is sheer terror," Oscar Wilde said. I had been driven anxiously to accomplish things, to learn, to be in the swirl of action, whatever that was. But now I was back to square one. Lying in my childhood bedroom, rethinking what to fear.

My mother had removed all vestiges of my life from this room. The fury and clutter were gone. The walls were softly white, hung with delicate water colors. The bedside lamp was a serene little antique. I stretched my arms up to the ceiling, interlocked my fingers, and hummed. How do you tell a man whom you barely know that you're planning to have his child? How do you explain that you have forged a link to this man—a lifelong connection, an intertwined lineage—without his permission? There must be some sort of protocol, somewhere. A useful script. It all seems so straightforward on the TV commercials: "Honey, the stick turned blue!"

"Yay!"

That's not going to work in this instance, is it? And yet, the only other conversation I'm familiar with is the special, grim one that all of my friends had in their twenties: "Listen . . . John . . . I missed my period."

"Oh God."

"I can't do this, I'm not ready."

"No."

"I think it's about three hundred dollars."

"Right."

That bare-bones script, which speaks nothing of what will be felt.

On soap operas, pregnancy always seems to be presented as a connivance. "Stay with me, Gerard, I love you."

"Don't lie to me, Susan. I happen to know that you're carrying Shane's baby."

What about an historic twist? I could get a friend to phone Calvin. "My lord, good tidings, the queen is with child."

"Madam, you make my heart glad. I shall have an heir."

Calvin hadn't mentioned pining for an heir, but you never knew with men. Perhaps I should go back to the old-fashioned novel.

"Calvin," I could say, gazing at him searchingly, "I feel faint."

"Well, that's not surprising," he'd say. "You drank twice your weight in beer last night. Have a Bloody Mary. Hair of the dog."

I gradually fell asleep on the soft, pale-green eider-down, listening to the reassuring murmur of *Canada at Five* downstairs on the kitchen radio. I dreamed that I ran over Liza Minnelli with my bike.

Half-baked Truths

"Cock-a-doodle-dooo . . ."

My cell phone. I looked wildly around for it, inadvertently swinging a clutch of beets into the pistachio-hued sweater set of an elderly woman standing behind me at the checkout counter of the Harvest Time market on Yonge Street. My mother and I were unloading our cart, having decided to make, if not sense of my predicament, at least a celebratory feast, and I had the beets in one hand and a bag of new potatoes in the other, with this fucking phone dingling like a rooster somewhere in my shoulder bag. I pulled it out and answered, so that the beets now dangled unbecomingly from my ear.

"Hello?"

"Ciao, Francesca!" It was Calvin, crackling down the line from Europe.

"Oh, Calvin, I can't talk, I'm just about to pay for some groceries."

"But I borrowed this phone," he protested, his voice wavering in and out through the static. "I've only got a minute. I'm in the Dolomites. We're playing in a ski lodge."

"But can't you phone me tomorrow? I'm in Toronto."

"I miss you!"

"I miss you too," I said, jamming a finger in my other ear and hunching over to block out the clamor of the market. My mother, cottoning on to who the caller was, bored holes in my head with her eyes. "You have to tell him," she hissed.

"I can't tell him *here*," I hissed back. The cashier, a scowling Polish man with a hamlike nose, gestured at the beets hanging limply from one side of my head and pointed at the counter.

"You can't tell me what?" asked Calvin, alert with curiosity. I looked around at the press of glaring strangers, all of whom wanted me to shut up and get on with my purchase, and counterpoised the weight of their opprobrium with my mother's burning eyes, which dared me to behave so childishly as to conceal a pregnancy from the father, at my age.

"I'm probably pregnant," I whispered into the phone, so quietly that even I couldn't hear myself. There was an infinite pause.

"Frannie, are you there?" he finally said. "You have to speak up. This cell phone's about as effective as a wooden shoe."

"I'm shopping for buns," I said stupidly, "because I've got one in the oven."

"You're making buns?" he asked, incredulous. "I didn't know you made buns."

"Oh, for God's sake—Puddies. Puddie buns. I've got Puddie buns in the oven. And I didn't—I needed more. How are you?"

"What the fuck are you talking about?"

Just then there was a blast of white noise down the line and I realized that we'd lost the connection. I pressed "end" and slammed my cell phone on the checkout counter. My mother, wholly unperturbed, paid for the groceries and handed me a bag.

"Don't be embarrassed," she said calmly, as we headed for the car. "Nobody had the faintest idea what you were saying."

Oh, fine. I felt like throttling her, I really did.

Last Days of the *Ancien Régime*

"Frannie," said The Editor, when I'd safely returned to his realm, "this is the great Michael Ignatieff."

The man in question, still stunning-looking in his fifties, was smiling easily at me and proffering his hand. We were at La Trattoria on Seventh Avenue for dinner. The sound of Italian ceramic clattered all around us as waiters bustled about with trays of antipasto and polenta. I was starving.

"Michael," rumbled The Editor, "may I present, in turn, my lovely associate editor and your fellow country-woman, Frannie Mackenzie."

Ignatieff hadn't lived in Canada in at least twenty years. Now he was an ex-pat in London, known in literary circles as the Thinking Woman's Crumpet, due to his frequent star turns mulling over the fate of the Balkans on the BBC. He had an air about him, a glamor, a grace, that made me wonder wistfully if I could benefit from my pregnancy glow without anyone actually concluding that I was pregnant.

"Ah," he said, teasingly, "you're the golden touch on my manuscript."

"Ah," I thought. Well, I was actually thinking two things simultaneously: (a) We were meant for each other, you and me, and (b) if someone doesn't get me some food, *right this instant,* I'm going to gnaw on the bloody table.

"I'm not a golden touch," I demurred. "Your writing is brilliant."

"It is that," conceded The Editor, scanning the menu through his bifocals. I suppose he didn't notice my swooning. The only libido he ever monitored was his own. The Editor had once gutturally muttered in my ear after an eleventh glass of Christmas-party champagne: "Frances, you fine, fiiiine woman, I find myself in-*eluch*tably sexually drawn to you," which I—not being a very competent opportunist—merely parlayed into an anecdote for soused friends.

"I've been musing about separatism in Quebec," Ignatieff ventured. "It's such a deeply unsettling *challenge* to the core of Canadian identity. It wasn't covered well here, I'm afraid. The subtleties of our political culture get lost in the translation."

"That's true," I said, nodding in agreement. I waved frantically at a waiter, who cocked his ear irritably as he passed by. "Bread?" I mouthed. He plunked down a loaf on his return pass.

Trying not to act feral, I devoured every piece of it but

two slices while Ignatieff described his recent trip to Montenegro. He was, I mused, everything that I'd ever dreamed suitable. Accomplished, bold, socially gracious, a touch mischievous, emotionally pent-up in a wonderfully provocative way. One could sense real excitement within that crumpet. I was half in love with him by the time he'd analyzed the Middle East and the tartuffo had arrived. Alas, I suddenly had to fall asleep.

"Gotta go home," I mumbled, struggling with immense effort to avert dropping my head into my dessert plate with a dull thud. My companions regarded me in surprise.

"But Frannie, certainly you can stay for coffee?" The Editor was not amused, for we were, as it happened, right in the middle of a discussion about Ignatieff's next assignment, and a question had just been put to me about whether an analysis of the Quebec crisis might be plausibly blended with a contemplation of the frictions in Kosovo. My brain was trying valiantly to stay in the game, but my body had other business to attend to, such as forming little toe bones, and was behaving as commandingly as a boot-camp sergeant, barking at me to drop and do twenty. You will fall sound asleep on my count, *is that clear?*

"Perhaps, if you'll excuse me, I'll just visit the washroom for a moment?"

"Of course," said Ignatieff, tilting his head deferentially. There was a settee in the vestibule of the woman's washroom. What if I just lay down for a second . . . ?

* * *

The next day, I called in sick, incredulous that I'd fallen asleep in the bathroom of a restaurant in the midst of a business meeting. And furthermore, I'd met the man of my dreams! A mere four months too late! What were the odds? Why is destiny so capricious? How could I even be thinking such things? I was a horse in midstream, that's what I was. Or, no, that couldn't be right. I stared out the window at the brick wall next door, which was all I had for a view, and tried to remember the correct expression. Changing horses in midstream. That was it, that's what I was doing. Still a single career girl. And yet, not. Not at all. A mom in a tent dress with her hair in a bun.

I sat down miserably on my unmade bed and stared sourly about at the material bits and pieces of my space, the dubious food on the kitchen counter, the piles of papers in my hall, snatches of Kleenex on the bathroom floor, shirts strewn about with sleeves flung up like the fallen figures of Pompeii. Someone like Michael Ignatieff wouldn't want me, anyway; he'd want a woman who effortlessly kept his home gracious. On my desk, I noted a Burger King drink cup with a straw jutting out of it, capped, for some reason, by the lid of a ball point pen. A light bulb. A fork. Three dimes, a cassette tape, some Post-it notes, a *Vanity Fair* magazine, and an empty Twinkies package.

To all this confusion I would now have to add a baby and her accoutrements: a welfare check, for instance. And a crib. Where would I put a crib? I'd have to dangle it from the ceiling. That wouldn't work, surely? Add diapers, booties, and bottles necessitating Diaper, Bootie, and Bottle Drawers, and—well—oh, bloody hell.

This was not going to work. I was going to have to move. I wasn't going to be rescued by Michael Ignatieff. By the time he handed in his manuscript, I'd be concealing my pregnancy with a barrel. *The Pithy Review* would terminate my contract. My career had been rising on spec. It would fall.

Day 17 without talking to Calvin. He kept sending me postcards conveying who-knows-what in utterly illegible handwriting. "F., how are you? I'm in [unintelligible] with Frank and [unintelligible]. You wouldn't [unintelligible] the [unintelligible]. XO Calvin."

The guy needed Cyrano de Bergerac. And fast. What we had here is a fine mess indeed.

What to Expect When You Fall Down a Well

My mother is a firm believer in the subconscious, which takes over, she says, "like a plane's computer when the pilot loses control."

"I hardly lost control," I snapped at her later. "You make it sound like I drank too much Kalhúa and drove my Pontiac into a stop sign."

"Give it your own interpretation, Frances. That's just my analysis."

All right, then. All right. I'd gone back to Toronto a few weeks after my dinner with Ignatieff for another doctor's appointment. Calvin had left a worrisome message on my voice mail about extending his trip, ostensibly to catch the Monterey Jazz Festival at the invitation of the Garden Snakes' new French promoter, Roxanne *Je ne Sais Who*—presumably of the small, *tout petit* breasts—and I was grappling with the revelation that our DNA was intimately acquainted, but we were not. Ignatieff had also left a message—a rather flirtatious one, I thought, and so I was suffering from a bit of cognitive dissonance. (Maybe he wouldn't mind raising the baby? or I could tell him she was his, albeit born very prematurely. I could paint his eyebrows on her . . .)

In Dr. Nandha's office, I heard the baby's heartbeat beneath my own. It was fast, like a small, frightened creature discovered hiding in the dark. Except that she wasn't frightened, she was moving about busily. Doctor Nandha kept getting a skipped beat on her Doppler. "D'you hear?" she asked, her face alight with engagement. "There, moved. . . . Moved again."

I grinned at the unexpected wonder of her, picturing the baby doing little somersaults, darting around like a silverfish. She was living her own life already! Except that she had to follow where I go, like we were differently sized Siamese twins. So here we went into the airport bar to await our return flight and order a glass of pinot grigio, looking quickly around in case there were some medically intuitive policemen about. I'll just have two fraught sips, oh my God that tastes like moonlight, just two, before reluctantly nudging the glass toward the bartender.

What's done is done, I reflected to myself: the booze I drank, the pot I smoked, the bad cold I slogged through, the cigarettes. Either she'd be a deaf-mute or she wouldn't. And if she was, well then I'd just tell her about Helen Keller. "See how much Helen Keller accomplished, sweetie?" I'd yell at her, gesticulating in Braille. "She was a deaf-blind-mute and she became famous!"

I gazed out the window at the taxiing planes and lectured myself. This was utterly speculative. She could be perfectly formed. Yet, perhaps, subtly brain-damaged, like a psychopath who grows up to shoot me for insurance money.

"Excuse me, can I have that pinot grigio back, actually?"

My mother never knew, until he arrived premature and stillborn, that her first son had been fatally ruined by the sulfa drugs she took to cure a kidney infection. Such small, innocuous-looking tablets, before bedtime each night for a week. Had he lived, I would still be an egg in her womb, my own baby never to be born. Those sulfa drugs saved our lives. The future Miss Lucy Mackenzie's and mine.

Think of that.

No, don't. Not now. Very bad idea, ruminating on the philosophical implications of life and death when you leave the bar and head for U.S. Customs and Immigration, where Inspector Callie Johnson, resident of Buffalo, newly transferred from her inaugural border post in the dehydrated migrant fields of Brownsville, Texas, was about to bellow *"Who the hell do you think you are?"*

Which began with me handing her my passport. "Where you headed?" asked Johnson, grabbing up the navy blue document and dragging it through her electronic gee-gaw.

"New York," I said, wondering if I had my apartment key with me, or if I had left it at my mother's.

"Where do you live?"

"Toronto." I corrected myself: "New York. I'm from Toronto but I live in New York at the moment."

"Are you working there?" She glanced up at me suspiciously.

"Oh, sort of." I rolled my eyes. "When I'm awake."

"May I have your work papers?"

"They're being updated." I smiled cooperatively. The truth, which I considered of minor importance, was that I hadn't ever quite gotten around to mailing in the visa renewal papers I was given by the magazine's lawyer, because I didn't have a stamp and then I forgot.

Inspector Johnson glared at me through her dark, thick-framed glasses. "Could you come this way, please, ma'am?"

Unnerved, I followed her to a small glass cubicle furnished with a clean white table and two chairs, where she motioned for me to sit down. I did, and was about to launch into an explanation when she turned on her crepe-soled heels and left the room. She did not return for half an hour, which I duly noted, minute for panicking minute, on the wall-mounted clock.

"What is the matter with you?" I burst out in dismay, upon her unsmiling return. "You just made me miss my plane!"

"I would advise you that you are speaking with a representative of the United States government, ma'am," she intoned, in that special, uninflected voice that cops use when they ask you to get out of your ve-hi-cle.

"And therefore what?"

"You do not argue with me, ma'am."

"Well, I'm sorry," I said, trying not to burst into tears, "but I'm hardly strangling old ladies with their nylons, am I? I just forgot to renew my visa application."

She had hair as thick and straight as straw, which jutted down to her shoulders. Her nose was short and stubby. Her mouth was mean. She was raring for a fight.

"You are currently unauthorized for employment in the United States," she stated flatly. "Do you have firearms or explosives in your possession, ma'am?"

I laughed, a little bark of surprise. "Yes I do, they're outside in my Ryder Truck ve-hi-cle."

"I'm going to ask you to surrender the keys."

"I'm just *joking*." I couldn't believe this woman, she was staring right through me. She was staring right through my life, and had the power to destroy it, and clearly didn't give a shit if she was talking to a person or a loaf of bread. "Of course I don't have firearms, I'm just a magazine editor."

"You are not an American citizen, and you are not entitled to edit an American magazine without a valid H-1 visa."

"I'm not *not* American," I said, shocked by her declaration. "My great-grandfather fought in the Civil War."

"Ma'am, I don't care who you are related to, you are not permitted past this border. As of now."

"Is this any way," I said, flailing about in a last hurrah of tremulous defiance, "to treat an expectant mother?"

Very ill-advised, bringing that up. If I were a man, I'd know how to make the sound of a slingshot being whipped out of a back pocket. *Ziiiinnnng.* She catapulted me out of the U.S. of A. without further ado.

Bloody hell.

God fucking damn it.

Shit on a bloody stick.

"Now calm down, Frances," my mother advised. "She was just being officious. It wasn't personal."

"She was a monster, a vicious ogre!"

"I thought the magazine's lawyer was arranging your visa," my mother said.

"He was!"

"Well then, what did the border woman object to?"

"She objected to the fact that I was a speck of dirt."

I was standing in my mother's living room, astounded that I was there, that I wasn't on a flight to La Guardia en route to a meeting with Michael Ignatieff to discuss tribalism in the Balkans.

My mother went into pace mode, gracefully circumnavigating the living room like a sailboat, now slowing, now speeding up, as if on little gusts of inspiration.

"I suppose the point is that you can't try a different port of entry and hope for better service," she said, "because she hung her threat on you telling fibs about your status." She lapsed back into thought. I sank onto her couch and sighed.

"I believe she said that if I tried to reenter the country on false pretenses, without clearing up my work permit, I'd be permanently banned."

She circled the room. "You may have to stay in Canada until you arrange for a visa, but the question is how long." At this, she crossed one arm across her chest and rested the other elbow upon her hand, the better to conduct in the air, as if thinking aloud to a roomful of students.

"So here is where we have a difficulty, Frances. It's now the month of July."

"No," I said, "it is not. It's June."

"All right, June. And you're due in December? If the paperwork drags out, you will return to New York and find yourself on the verge of being unfit to work, but in all likelihood unable to take maternity leave, and in no position to pay for your delivery at, for example, St. Vincent's where, by the way, your Aunt Blossom gave birth to Violet for the cost of a house." She stopped pacing and absently rearranged two pictures on the mantelpiece. "I think the only sensible thing is to stay here."

"What are you saying?" I asked miserably. "That I take my 'confinement' in Toronto?"

"Yes, I think so, I do. It's the only rational response. Work it through, Frances. Your apartment isn't suitable for a baby. Your, your . . ." She trailed off, trying to remember Calvin's name. "Your friend has no money. Pregnancy is a time of rest, Frances, it's not a good time in your life to face challenging tasks."

"Why not?" I argued. "Look at pioneer women. They marched across the Rockies when they were pregnant as barns. I'd say a mountain range full of bears and alligators is a lot more daunting than a paperwork scuffle."

She ignored me. "Have your baby in a supportive environment and resume your career in New York when you're ready."

"No!" I burst out. "This is ridiculous! One night of inadequate birth control and I'm banished to the provinces?

And to where? Where am I supposed to go? To a home for unwed mothers?"

My mother looked worriedly toward the vestibule and I followed her gaze. My father was standing there, obscured by the shadows of late afternoon; he wore his straw boater, and was perspiring from his cycle to the library.

"Well now, Freddie, don't shout." Oh, my father. My father was very tender. He'd entered a shop full of snorting bulls like a porcelain figurine who'd gotten lost. He had an upside-down mouth, apprehensive and appeasing. I couldn't bring him into this conversation.

"I'm hungry," I announced, and hastily departed, leaving it up to my mother.

My father had nicknamed me in honor of Frideric Handel, and spent most of his time, when not being an accountant, listening to classical music and reading "what to read" books. He absorbed the news as if presented with a vexing riddle. I found him sometime later lying on his favorite old couch, feet crossed at the ankles, gazing into the air with his bushy ginger eyebrows knit in thought. "Well now, Freddie," he said in his soft Scottish burr, having heard me descend the stairs, "I've been thinking about your situation, and I wonder if you know that your brother is looking for someone to care for his house while he and Penny set themselves up in London."

"No," I said, profoundly uninterested. "I didn't know that."

"Please don't use that tone," he countered, sounding hurt. It's so easy to hurt my father's feelings. You could

blow on him and he'd assume that look of sanctimo-
nious, held-in pain.

"It might work very well," he persisted. "There
wouldn't be anything as committing as a lease. You could
just haunt the place for as long as you needed. David's
leaving next week, and Penny keeps vetoing prospective
tenants. I imagine your brother is beginning to feel a bit
desperate."

Having made this case, he tucked his fists under his
chin and resumed staring into space. He did not mention
a grandchild, or an absent son-in-law, or my collapsed
editorial ambitions, in which he'd taken such vicarious
pleasure. He solved a small, pragmatic issue as if filling
in one crossword puzzle clue, all the more satisfactory
for addressing both of his children—my brother splayed
Across, my own self Down—and in this way accomplished as much as he could manage for the day.

Away in the Manger

Days of bereavement and quiet in my unexpected exile, desperately resentful of the baby, who cared not a wit and made me retch at the smell of martinis when I'd prefer to be drunk, draping myself across a chaise-longue. Yearning for New York, which had been stolen away from me like a mirage; pining for my afternoons in Central Park, for my evenings at the Ear, for that gregarious lunatic dressed in tin foil who always showed up on the subway. Craving my work, and the Temple Bar, and the chocolate cupcakes at the corner deli at 11th and Fifth, and my life, which had rhythm and quickness and current, not this stillness, not this listening to the rustle of the *Times Literary Supplement* downstairs at my father's round oak table and that's it, all other dialogues quiet, all aspirations derailed.

"I'm afraid I can't make the meeting tomorrow," I had

said to The Editor on the day I was banished, after first debriefing Marina.

"Understood," he said, "not a crisis. When can I expect you?"

"Well, Thursday's out, and Friday doesn't look too promising. How about never, is never good for you?"

He chuckled. I was quoting his favorite *New Yorker* cartoon. "Look," I continued, "the problem is that I got bounced at the border by some immigration freak on a power trip, and I don't know how long it's going to take me to sort it out."

The notion of capricious border guards abusing their power caught his fancy, and sent him on a ruminative flight about politics and prejudice that would, I realize, culminate in next month's essay. In the meantime, he lost interest in what I was actually saying and passed my conundrum off to the managing editor. "She can e-mail you the two pieces you're slated to tackle this issue."

"Stop behaving as if you've got the vapors," my mother said a week later, offering me a ham sandwich as I sat on the barstool at the kitchen counter, flipping listlessly through *Psychoanalytic Approaches to the Maternal Self*.

"You ought to go and see your brother."

"I can't move into his place," I said. "It would be humiliating. Absolutely not."

My brother and I are not close. We ought to be, since we're near to each other in age, and share a deep nostalgia for Monty Python movies, Tin-Tin comics, and Cat Stevens. But I shun him. He pelted me with rolled-up socks throughout my childhood, dangled me by my ankles from the porch railing, frequently made me crawl gauntlets of pillows on some tarted-up pretext of deserved punishment, and once tried to cook me in the oven.

Partly it is that—the smug glee with which he tortured me in my formative years—that makes me tense up in his presence, and partly it is the fact that he cannot open his fleshy, grinning mouth without insulting me. I did not wish to live in his house because I knew exactly what kind of hay he would make of my disaster, and he made it the instant I knocked on his door.

"Hey, Miss Cool Thang," he drawled, jutting his head out of his renovated Victorian house in gentrified Cabbagetown later that day. "Aren't we the damsel in distress."

He clutched a crystal tumbler full of bourbon, which was typical, and was decked out in white dress pants so filmy that you could see the ungainly outlines of his back pockets and the tuck of his shirt, which sported green and white stripes like a restaurant mint. He grinned, to show me that his barb was all in fun, and then leaned in for a hug. "Penny is just thrilled for you," he confided. "You know how hard it is for her, discovering that her tubes are blocked, and then you just lie drunk in New York for a couple a years and presto! Unwed Mommy time!" He chuckled, "fun-ly," and slapped me on the back. "C'mon in."

I followed him through the foyer, which was the size of my entire apartment. If what I had in New York was a necessary niche in the larger, more vibrant world that engaged me, my brother's house was his castle. He'd come into money through a dot.com venture, and then lavished it on a fantasy of himself as a rich guy. Here I am! Rich! Fun!

I don't know what he was aiming for precisely, but he somehow came across as a Miami Beach fag circa Versace's '90s. The sitting room he led me into was painted black and criss-crossed with steel shelves, upon which he'd arranged steel-framed photographs just so: David on vacation in Palm Beach in an orange Speedo; David and Penny nervously astride horses at a Wyoming Dude Ranch; the two of them waving from the deck of some cruise ship off Bermuda; in front of the Park Plaza in New York.

All this self-adoration complemented by black leather chairs, an ultramodern steel table, and a faux zebra skin carpet.

"It isn't real," he chortled, following my gaze. "It's a Starck."

"Starck?" I asked, bemused.

"The designer," he said.

"Ah."

I was drawn to the potted plants throughout the room, which appeared to be glinting steel bowels filled with grass.

"That's not grass, is it David?"

"That would, in fact, be grass," he said, tinkling the ice cubes in his bourbon and smiling. "The guy I hired to design it said the room was too severe for flowers."

"So you're accenting it with grass."

"I kinda like it."

I pondered the bowls for a moment and suddenly worried: "Am I supposed to mow this grass, or . . . or what?"

"You know, you're going to have to ask Penny that, Frannie. I don't tend the shrubbery in these parts."

"Okay, well . . ." I shrugged. Whatever. Grass. I'll just stick it outside.

"So this is my lair," David said, "and if you could not come in here, that would be my ideal scenario. I'll show you the main living room, which is Penny's lair."

We moved into a room that overwhelmed me with its explosion of color. The walls were papered all over in two-toned stripes of fuschia and red; the ceiling was turquoise blue, and the furniture consisted of huge, overstuffed couches featuring fuschia begonias against skyblue silk next to low tables all of glass, with gilded legs. The whole space was crowded with folk-art animal statues and crystal unicorns.

"What a hullabaloo," I said.

"Penny likes to cheer herself up," my brother answered, pointedly and ambiguously. I was left to puzzle out that one. Did she need cheering up because she was married to a pompous fool? Or because his promiscuously fecund sister was about to loaf about in her special lair?

"This is very personal to her," David added, "this room, so I would appreciate it if you generally didn't hang out in here."

"Okay," I said, trying to be cooperative, wondering if I'd be made to sleep in the garden shed.

"Where is Penny?" I had not seen my sister-in-law since the night that we all attended a gala fund-raising dinner at the Four Seasons Hotel on behalf of UNICEF, of which my mother was a devoted supporter. Penny had come along to bask in the faint starlight thrown by Jane Fonda, who was accompanying her keynote speaker husband and desperately trying to avoid women like Penny by pretending to be riveted by the second-rate Inuit art that festooned the ballroom walls. As Ted Turner ambled through his old war story about tossing one billion dollars at the UN to cover American debt, Penny sat ramrod-straight in her sleeveless silver Dior gown, staring despondently into her soup bowl, a fat choker of pearls glimmering at her neck, her sharply cut hair meeting at the point of her heart-shaped chin. All dressed up amidst do-gooding fuddy-duddies.

"Where is she?" echoed David, who was investigating a water stain on his pants. "She's with her personal efficiency consultant."

"No way!" I laughed in delight.

He glared at me, and then as quickly assembled his wolfish, patronizing smile, as if we'd never been children together, and I'd never seen him scared.

"The man is exclusive," he reassured me. "He's counseled Fortune 500 executives."

I stared at him. "Oh David, you know, can't you make a donation to the Salvation Army or something? Do you have to throw every cent at affectation?"

"Well, that's just merry bullshit coming from you," he retorted. "What's more grandiose than to assume you can be homeless, jobless, and manless and just pop out a child prodigy on my doorstep?"

That was it. We'd wounded each other fatally. He stormed off to the Mediterranean-tiled kitchen to pour himself an Armagnac and I stalked toward the door.

"Forget it," I called. "I'll stay somewhere else."

"Do that," he shouted. Then he came scuttling anxiously down the corridor. "Wait, I haven't made any other arrangements for Kevin."

"Who's Kevin?" Frightening notions flew through my mind. Penny's uncle in the attic. A deranged cosmetician in the basement.

"My dog, my dog," he grumbled. "My fucking dog."

I raised my brows. "I didn't know you had a dog."

He waved at the backyard. "He's not allowed in the house. He sheds."

Curious, I walked back to the kitchen and peered out the sliding glass doors. There, on a white plastic patio chair, was a golden-haired dog in a deep sulk, with his muzzle hanging over the edge of the chair—his huge brown eyes staring at nothing. My brand-new heart—that throbbing, oversensitive maternal one deep within my chest—broke instantly. "All right. I'll stay."

Dog comes in. Grass goes out.

A Brief Note About
Looking After a Dog

If you take him for a run while on your sister-in-law's bicycle and insist on holding on to his leash as you pedal, he will heedlessly bolt off at a ninety-degree angle in pursuit of a cat, and you will almost break your nose on the asphalt that flies up to greet you.

If you tie him up outside Daniel et Daniel Catering and disappear inside for half an hour to load up on fruit tarts and chicken, you must not forget that he is there when you reemerge to trundle off down the street, leaving him to sit patiently on the sidewalk for several hours until you slap your forehead in remembrance.

When you walk him, you must bring a baggie, lest you find yourself attempting to pick up his poop with a Starbucks coffee container lid because six people in Riverdale Park are staring at you, then at his bowel movement, and then back at you. It is an adjustment. It takes time. But you let him sleep in the bed because you have love to give, and he is warm, and breathes softly, and yips in his sleep.

I Know How Men in Exile
Feed on Dreams

—AESCHYLUS

There followed an interlude in my life that I shall think of ever after as banishment, even though I had returned to my family and the city of my birth. I was outside of my life, and could neither carry on living the old one, nor yet begin anew. My father, who was unnerved by my predicament, nonetheless was pleased to have my company, and talked at me endlessly about the books he was reading while I sat cross-legged in his study, sighing and editing the pieces I'd been sent from *The Pithy Review*. My mother was my mother, distant and skeptical and smoothly protective. She swiftly hooked me up with a friend of hers at *Toronto Life* magazine, knowing full well that I'd run out of cash sometime soon, and otherwise kept to her own schedule, which mostly consisted of listening, with mounting impatience, to her therapy patients, whom she categorized as the worried well.

"If their crises are so boring, then why do you do it?" I asked her.

"Because I'm good at it," she replied briskly. "I make them stop all this worrying and just get on with their lives."

Of course, I was worried, and she knew it, and I knew that she knew it, but neither of us wished to discuss my particular worry. My father ignored it as well, because he couldn't approach the implications with any sort of insight and preferred to spout irrelevant quotations from Alan Bloom. Calvin had gone AWOL, and was doubtless surrounded by dancing girls. Or maybe he was pining for me, which was equally frightening. I seesawed between need and resistance when I thought about him, and had nothing coherent to say to Marina when she phoned worriedly for updates. My future, which dictated the drift of my present, was peculiarly unmentionable. All I could do for the time being was to focus on mundane adventures.

One day, I had a root canal and then decided to go bra shopping, just to see if it would be more pleasurable or less. Most women, and I think I can generalize here, will put off buying a new bra until their straps disintegrate, and even then they might improvise for a while. Wear sweatshirts, for instance, or simply not leave the house. This is because bra shopping is exceedingly dull. What are bras, if not bland, ineffectual necessities tarted up with an array of sewn-on daisies? The most timid fashion statement I have ever known is the teensy, superfluous bow at the cleavage of my bra, intended to suggest . . . I don't know what. A certain hypermodest girlish femininity. "Hey, naughty boy, look at me in my sagging, fraying, beige-colored, oversized bra. Bet ya didn't notice the bow."

Ideally, you want to be able to buy bras like widgets at the hardware store. You just want to snatch them up and slap them on the checkout counter, because that's about as interesting as they are to you as a shopping activity. But no, instead you have to try fifteen varieties on, because none of them ever fit, and after the third one, you start thinking about what a big hog you are as you stand before a rudely unflattering mirror. Then the whole exercise becomes a harsh combination of boring and humiliating and you must stifle the urge to bolt.

I wandered into a chic little boutique in Yorkville called the Bra Bar, a place I remembered from the panicked days before my sister's wedding in 1990, when it was incumbent upon me to find a strapless, backless bra for my bridesmaid dress, which is just the ultimate act of wishful thinking. What I was really looking for was some quick breast-reduction surgery. What the Bra Bar sold me were "support cups." Support cups are basically shoulder pads for your breasts, which you stick on with something much, much more adhesive than masking tape. They support nothing at all, really. But just try—I defy you—to remove them. When I put my cups on a few days before the wedding to try out the look, I wound up having to spend the night in them, and then the next day, and another night, until I finally located some sort of solvent that could loosen the adhesive without skinning me alive.

What else the Bra Bar sells is hard to discern, since all merchandise is tucked into little glass drawers behind the sales counter, as if you were in an apothecary. You therefore have no choice but to resort to assistance if you want to exit with a purchase.

I timidly requested some samples of the Wonderbra and headed for the fitting room, only to be confronted in the mirror with three variations on the theme of droop. I could droop straight down like I was aiming two bombs at China, or instead droop at a weird, planing angle as if somebody mistook me for a sofa cushion and sat on my bust. Or alternatively, my flesh could droop out the sides, which was just really, really attractive and made me proud.

"Can I help you?" the salesclerk inquired when I reemerged. *No, you may not.*

Undeterred, she asked me to consider the latest rage, which were those terrifying foam breast pods designed to disguise your own breasts entirely, and to replace them with a sort of false-storefront effect of perfect, round, nipple-free orbs. Have you seen these? They turn you into Barbie. I think they're available all the way up to size 32A.

"Are you mad?" I asked her. "I'm pregnant."

"Oh," she said, offering me a solicitous compliment: "I didn't notice."

"Well, I am, and I think I should just get a couple of those open-flap things for breastfeeding, I don't know what you call them."

"Nursing bras."

"Right. Just . . . just . . . can I have two Wonderbra nursing bras?"

"What size?" She glanced furtively at my chest.

"Oh God," I sighed. "I don't know. One medium and one jumbo."

Back outside, heat shimmered on the pavement as tourists and rich Torontonians milled up and down Yorkville Avenue in search of the glittery trinkets on offer in the little boutiques. I stood squinting in the glare of afternoon light, and let a Mercedes nose past on the crowded street before crossing over to the hot-dog stand in front of the Four Seasons Hotel. "Hot today, isn't it?" I said to the vendor, who was an East Indian fellow in a paper hat.

"No," he disagreed. "It isn't. It isn't hot."

"All right." I regarded him pensively for a moment. "I'd like an all-beef hot dog, please." I had just dropped a large amount of relish on my shoe and was bending over in a fluster to wipe it away when he grabbed me from behind. Two large hands at the waist. I startled, and then he took my free hand and lifted it above my head, twirling me around. What was this? Had the vendor gone insane? But it wasn't him. It was Evan.

"Evan!" He danced me around the hot-dog stand. "I knew it was you," he said, delighted. Evan, my great love. I hadn't seen him in years. He was still so beautiful. Long-limbed and broad-shouldered, graceful, with quizzical blue eyes. Only now he was attired in an elegant suit and looked decidedly moneyed. I guessed he'd gone into law, after all that fretting.

"So what's up with you, Frannie?" He appraised me. "You look plump and content. I heard you've hit your stride in New York." There was so much emotional weight in those two sentences, he might as well have hurled a cannonball at my chest. Weight in what he intended, weight in what he didn't know. I flashed an unconvincing little smile and shrugged. He reached for my hot dog, loosened it from my hand and ate half in one bold bite. Then he took hold of my elbow and led me to a nearby bench in the Yorkville "parkette," which was surrounded by potted lavender.

"Go on," he said, lowering me by pressing lightly on my shoulders. "Sit down, take a minute out of a hot day, and catch me up on your life." He was always so thrillingly in charge.

Now I threw him off-stride. "I'm having a baby, how's that?"

He arched his brows in surprise and whistled. "No shit."

A little wave of silence washed over us. It could have been his baby, of course. He understood that. A memory flashed through my mind of the moment I walked into Evan's house on the night of his twenty-fifth birthday and found him sitting at his borrowed table in the kitchen, which was littered with plates of half-eaten toast, wine bottles gnarled with candle wax, unpaid electric bills. His broad back was clothed in a white dress shirt for the play we were going to see, and his fist was clenched to his chin, I remember, as if he were struck by some notion. A birthday card I'd sent him was sitting upright on the table. I said: "What are you thinking about?"

"I'm thinking about how lucky I am that I met you."

Maybe he went on to say that to all the girls. So much love spilled, so carelessly and staining, like beer on a frat-house floor.

He bought himself a hot dog and we talked about my situation, which I somehow translated into an account of being married to the king of jazz, very famous, with whom I was shortly having a baby in Tribeca. The sun was making my head hot. I reached up absently to place my palm flat against my hair and bounce it lightly. "What about you, Evan?" I asked.

"Oh, frolics, hijinks, masterful accomplishments, that sort of thing."

He never answered straight. Just always with that "dare ya" grin on his face. "I suppose I'm getting married in September."

I didn't want to know. "To who?"

"No one you've met," he said. Of course not. "She works in my firm."

His cell phone rang just then, and he had it out and at his ear in a beat, with his usual restless agility. I waited for a while, and then I rose. I didn't want to overhear anymore of his new life, with its intimate, unknowable inflections. He gestured at me with a commanding wave to sit down again, to wait, but I didn't want to wait. "See you," I mouthed, and merged myself into the flow of the summer crowd. On the subway, I hummed a Paul Simon song. "Maybe I'm obliged to defend every love, every ending, or maybe there's no obligation now."

Head tilted against the window as the subway rattled

northward through the city, thinking about Evan, about how much more familiar he was to me than the man whose child was inside me.

I followed him to Mexico once, long after we'd broken up, but not long after we'd last slept together, holding our breath, withholding our promises, saying maybe this matters, maybe it doesn't. I took this last, bold gambit, installing myself in a house in Cuernavaca when I learned he had gone down to Mexico for a spell, waiting at a careful distance for him to come, and to fall to his knees. He called from his flat in Mexico City to make some arrangements, and when I hung up, the housekeeper regarded me curiously.

"Is the American your boyfriend?" she asked, having answered the phone.

"Well, he . . ." Uh-oh. Cultural divide. "He was once."

"You aren't married . . ."

"No."

"You are how old, *señorita*?"

"Twenty-nine."

She gazed at me, bemused.

He arrived at the gate in a 1981 Mustang, his passenger seat strewn with pistachio shells. Stooping out of the car, he stood there blinking, his eyes the same teal shade as his sweater. He looked drained, and a little disoriented. But when we linked hands, there was the familiar feeling of connection. He smiled, and I set about my mission. I thought if I could introduce him to me newly . . . Read this, this is a book I'm touched by; listen to the music I like; notice, on my dresser, letters from people

PLAYING HOUSE

who love me. These are the gaps to be filled to rejoin us completely. He drank margaritas, and listened and watched, and after a while he sheepishly announced that he had a new girlfriend, a Mexican woman named Lupe.

He mused uncertainly about her significance to him, lost in rationalizations, heartbreaking for having to hedge so much about whether she mattered. We climbed into his Mustang and drove into the hills. The land was harsh. Farmers were trying to grow stalks of corn in a film of dust. Starved cows and mules rooted around the roadside, chewing on thorns and scraps of plastic.

"You keep making these jabbing little remarks," he said. I know I was. My anger was wild and futile. If he makes no promises you have no means to feel betrayed.

We were heading for Los Grutas, caves a mile deep, one hundred feet high, fashioned by subterranean rivers. The Mustang squealed around a final hairpin turn and we reached the state park entrance where, for a few pesos, we could leave the light and dust behind. From the mouth of the cave, we could see stalagmites towering up on either side of a slippery, twisting trail lit by yellow flood-lights. Without people or trees, you lost your sense of scale, and could imagine the cave as a mythical world, goblins on the trail ahead. Stalagmites rose up like grotesque statues, witches and demons, casting distorted shadows on the rock wall. Stalactites projected downward from the cavern ceiling like giant animal fangs and jagged spears.

We got ahead of the guide, leaving his flashlight behind. Evan strode faster than I, and all at once I lost him in the shadowy pitch of an underpass between stalagmite and cavern wall. After a silence, he whistled, but it echoed and came from everywhere. There was a fork in the trail, I didn't know which path he'd taken. And I thought: *This is where we'll always be. Ex-lovers navigating through darkness like bats do, guided by emotional echoes, now sensing, now losing the warmth.*

How many years you waste that way, waiting for love to take hold.

The subway approached Summerhill Station. I got up and moved, a bit wobbly, toward the doors. Me and a couple of university kids, who were holding hands, hip and graceful, unaware what love was, I'd guess. Too innocent to see how it was about to set them loose in a maze.

The Element of Surprise

Cockadoodledoo . . .

"Hello?"

"Where are you?" Calvin asked, eager and present.

I was actually in my now-absent brother's backyard on a humid afternoon, reading *What to Expect When You're Expecting*, and wondering why pregnancy books all refer to women's stomachs as "tummies," as if being pregnant regressed you to the age of five.

"Oh," I said vaguely, unwilling to get thrown into my banishment that precipitously, "I'm around and about, you know . . . where are you?"

"I'm home. I got home last night."

"Wow," I said, overwhelmed by his casual sense of where home was. "God, six weeks! Where do we start? Did you have a good time?"

"Did you get my postcards?"

"I did."

"Well, yes, I did have a good time."

I paused, waiting for elaboration.

None came. Okay. He could have won a million dollars at the casinos in Monte Carlo and run off with Roxanne to her French chateau. Or been stabbed. Maybe I was already supposed to know this.

"I missed you," he offered.

I stood up, invigorated by long-suppressed anger. "Oh, no, no, no, Calvin, you missed an idealized version of me, let me tell you. You missed the me who swans around Manhattan in sleek dresses and cavorts with the literati and sips martinis, and—"

"No," Calvin interrupted, "I missed the you who sleeps with your hand clutching your chin like a toppled-over Rodin, and the you who kissed me in the Cloisters with that minty-tasting lipstick on last winter, and the you who thought the song, 'Smoke on the water, fire in the sky' actually went: 'Slow-talkin' Walter, fire engine guy.' "

I felt equal parts forlorn and furious. I needed to tell him that everything had changed, and the woman he missed wasn't there anymore, her stomach had become a tummy, and he was a dolt for not knowing somehow; he had to know, because he had to share this. He was a witness to my gone but not forgotten self.

In my agitation I began to pluck buds from Penny's rosebush and sling them across the patio. "Calvin, things have changed since you were gone."

"Oh," he said, as if sobered by an unexpected punch.

"I don't mean what you think I mean," I said. "I just mean there have been a few developments in my life."

"Like what?" he asked, careful.

"Well, I've been booted out of New York by U.S. Immigration, and I'm house-sitting for my brother. And I'm pregnant."

There was a pronounced silence. "Get outta town," he finally said.

"I am." A bud whizzed through the air and bounced off Kevin's back as he lay dozing in the shade. "I am out of town. I'm in Ulan fucking Bator with nothing to do but cut my brother's house grass." More silence.

"Who did you get pregnant with?"

I laughed in surprise. He couldn't, or wouldn't, presume that it was him? I had dreaded many scenarios in this announcement, but not that.

"Calvin, it's yours."

Into the ensuing quiet I threw my defense, often rehearsed in these weeks. "I'm sorry. I'm not having an abortion. I'm thirty-three, I can't. I just can't."

"You don't need to say you're sorry, Frannie. We'll manage." He fell silent again, like my mother had. There were so many questions.

"I heard the heartbeat," I offered, encouragingly.

"You're kidding." He was roused from his reverie by that.

"So, I'm going to be a dad." A hint of pleasure in his voice?

"Yes," I said, and I was suddenly shaking, as if all the muscles in my body had tensed when I braced for this confession, and were just now relaxing. "Yes, you are."

He was sitting on the stone stairs leading up to the front door when I got home from shopping that weekend, gazing in puzzlement at the shrubbery. Penny had cottoned on to the idea of hedges clipped to resemble fantastical animals, like those she'd seen at villas in Italy; but she had no pruning experience and had fucked it up. Some of the hedges, if you squinted, were suggestive of bison, but most of them looked as if they'd been hacked at by the Jack Nicholson character in *The Shining*. A gardener was supposed to be coming to fix it.

Calvin had a black duffel bag with him, and also his Dobro. The air of New York was all about him in the casually elegant brogues he was wearing, the cut of his jeans, the funky shirt. I had forgotten that he was quite attractive. In my mind's eye, these past weeks, he'd acquired buck teeth and a Shriner's fez. All at once, I remembered my own outfit and ducked behind the maple tree at the foot of the garden. Nervously, as if staring down from a ledge, I let my eyes fall to the depths below and confirmed my suspicions that I was, in fact, still wearing sausage-legged sweatpants stolen from David's drawer and a pair of brown clogs. *I can't,* I thought. *He'll run away.*

Fuck, fuck, fuck . . .

I darted into the neighbors' yard, duck-walked along their fence, clambered over, and rushed to unlock the kitchen door. Inside, Kevin barked madly. I looked around wildly, as if fashionable clothes would miraculously appear out of the Tupperware. *Oh bloody*—I ran downstairs to my basement room, the one David had permitted me to stay in, provided I wore a sealed and helmeted suit supplied by the Centers for Disease Control, and rummaged around frantically in my things. Sandwich wrappers, pregnancy books, a bottle of folic acid. I discovered some black parachute pants that I could wear if I left them unzipped, and my new bra—my nursing bra!—and . . . fuck. I grabbed a bath towel and ran back upstairs to open the door.

"Hello," I said, smiling.

"Ah, Francesca." He smiled in turn, the lines at his blue-green eyes crinkling. "Look at you. Barefoot and pregnant in the Villa Disperato."

I was glad to see him, so very glad, and the afternoon melted away, towel becoming a blanket, in the gold-green light of evening in my brother's little garden.

"You don't have to stay," I said bravely, as we sat eating tomato sandwiches in the kitchen that night.

"Yes I do," he replied. "I'm not a cad."

"Don't stay out of obligation," I argued. "That would be insulting." He put down his sandwich, wiped his hands on his jeans, and leaned across the table to wipe mustard off my chin.

"I want to be with you." He paused. "Ideally, I wouldn't have to be with you in a family way quite yet, but so what? Life is not neat." He studied me for a moment. "And yes, there's obligation, of course there is. If nobody had a sense of obligation, nothing would have meaning. It would just be anarchy. I don't like anarchy anymore." He drummed his fingers on the table. "We're just going to have to figure it out." He said this simply and stubbornly. It was a vow he'd already made to himself, I realized.

I thought about Michael Ignatieff, the could-have-been, and Evan, the once-was, and then, as if for the first time, fully contemplated Calvin. I watched him in the slanting light, the way his hair fell over one eye, the set of his jaw, the tomato seed at the corner of his mouth, the way he was looking at me, seeking affirmation, trusting. I chewed on my thumbnail. You don't find the one, do you? The best one, the Perfect One. You just keep running like Wil E. Coyote and all of a sudden you're off the cliff. You fall into your life with the man who is running beside you.

The Way to a Man's Heart

Calvin isn't speaking to me because I served Tuna Helper for dinner last night. He's walking around in a state of despondent shock, wondering if this is what life has truly come to. Fake sauce with dehydrated parsley flakes. Father, father, why have you forsaken me? It took me twenty-four hours to determine that Tuna Helper was actually the issue. Until then I thought it was something I'd said, although I couldn't imagine what. He'd walked into the kitchen at dinnertime in a buoyant mood after jamming all afternoon with some musician friends he'd scared up at The Cameron on Queen Street. He kissed me behind the ear as I stood at the stove, and grabbed a Beck's from the fridge.

"What's up, little family?"

I didn't answer. I was listening to the news on the radio. The dog was poised at the foot of the stove, head down, alert as a runner about to bolt from his blocks. He instantly gobbled each scrap I dropped as if he hadn't eaten in three weeks.

"Kevin's far better than a Dirt Devil," Calvin observed. He sat down and drummed on the table, singing a blue-grass ditty. "My uncle used to love me but she died / chicken doesn't taste good unless it's french-fried."

I served him the noodles, which I'd tarted up with peas and a bit of salad. "What is this?" he asked, study-ing his plate. He glanced around the kitchen and spied the Tuna Helper box.

"You made that?"

"I did, yeah." What I did not do was register his shock, because I was trying to catch the weather report at the end of the news. I sat down and ate, the baby kicked, the dog gobbled. Calvin poked at his salad, then pushed his plate away with infinite sadness and drifted down into the basement to polish his marimba.

"Oh, for God's sake," I said this morning, after eking the problem out of him. He'd been sitting on the couch with one jeaned leg crossed over the other, arms hanging limply, gazing out the window at the rain. "What differ-ence does it make? It's just food."

"It's not just food," he said wanly. "It's what my mother used to make."

Of course this has to be about his mother. What if his lover turns into his mother? What fresh hell then?

"Calvin!" I protested. "We don't have any money! We can't keep eating takeout from Daniel et Daniel."

He sighed. Barely audible. Just a little whiffle through

the nose. "I don't know why I bought the Tuna Helper," I reflected, reaching for his unresponsive hand. "I saw it at Loblaws and something just came over me." Maybe Betty Crocker implants some sort of sonic device in Tuna Helper boxes that emit a scarcely detectable siren call to women. " 'Buy meeeee . . . I only take one brain cell and one pot. And if I get fed to the dog, who cares? I'm only Tuna Helper.'

"It was a lapse in judgment," I allowed. "I apologize, but it has nothing to do with turning into your mother."

It has a great deal to do with turning into my mother, though. My mother produced endless vats of Tuna Helper throughout my childhood. She also served Hamburger Helper and Pork Helper and God knows what else, Vegetable Helper, probably. I seem to recall a casserole concocted from Minute Rice, Campbell's Tomato Soup, and Cheez Whiz. My mother had no interest in cooking. She would stick anything in the oven—it could be a pair of shoes, really, or the spice rack—and simply hope that a dinner somehow materialized as she sat in her armchair in the den, reading *The Nature of Anxiety* by Rollo May.

We children eventually began to compensate for her adamant disinterest by becoming cooks ourselves. This was rather an ad hoc process, so that we tended to evolve specialties according to whim. Annabelle made nothing but cakes—wild, sumptuous, fruity cakes with meringue or chocolate liqueur glaze. She would burst triumphantly through the swinging door from the pantry into our airy dining room and place her latest creation on the dining-room table with authoritative precision. "Oh wow," we'd all say. "Bravo."

As Annabelle's popularity in high school waxed and waned, she began to invest her self-esteem in her cakes. They got more and more elaborate, and increasingly vulnerable to being dropped as she swung open the pantry door. "Fuck!" she would scream, when the double-chocolate mousse cake with whipped-cream sculpture slipped and soundlessly exploded on the floor shortly after a boy broke up with her. Then she would run up to her bedroom and slam the door so hard, with such damn-you-all finality, that the paintings trembled on the wall.

After that, she made curries. Beef curry, lentil curry, cauliflower balti, curried chicken salad, cocktail wiener korma, whatever. As long as she could sprinkle turmeric and garam masala into her pots, she felt happy and self-actualized. She had fallen in love with India after a monthlong visit to New Delhi with the Indian ambassador's daughter, a pixie-faced girl named Zarina who attended our school. She returned in a silk vermilion sari, with blue glass bangles jingling at each wrist, on a bitterly cold February day. I remember her picking her way through the snow bank that flanked our driveway with a look of crestfallen sorrow. (After some weeks of despair, she decided to run away to Bombay. She pinned a note to my mom's new Margaret Atwood novel: "My heart says stay, but my feet say go, go, go." She made it as far as Hamilton.)

David, who spent the vast majority of his time smoking pot in his bedroom and painting wounds on his plastic soldiers with Annabelle's Cerise nail polish when he wasn't torturing me, grew weirdly accomplished at roasting meat. He presided in uncommunicative silence over turkeys and chickens and sides of lamb, invariably serving them with roughly chopped root vegetables.

I, being the youngest and least called-upon cook, developed a knack for preparing cakes the size of cocktail coasters with an Easy-Bake oven. My repertoire only expanded when I moved to New York and fell under the spell of Zabar's and Dean & Deluca, whereupon I began experimenting with Peruvian blue potatoes and tapenade. When Calvin and I weren't eating like surprised royalty in my flat, we were dining on steak fries at Lucky Strike or black-bean soup at El Teddy's in Tribeca. This is what Calvin had come to associate with love: cool food, nonchalantly acquired, shared with a woman in a fetching chartreuse dress. How brief that romance was. How elusive it seemed to him now.

"Come on, don't put this kind of pressure on me," I complained. "Am I, or am I not, supposed to be maternal? Well, this is my maternal conditioning. You might as well get used to it, because the baby isn't going to eat beet gnocchi with lemon sauce. She's going to slingshot it around the room and ask for a cracker."

I knew this because I'd been making a close, apprehensive study of motherhood in the guise of Ellie and her little son, Lucas. We'd just been down to the beach together that morning, to which Ellie arrived—I noted with interest—with a large supply of organic beet chips, tuna sandwich squares, sliced vegetables, dried apple pieces, mango juice, sunblock, beach toys, and unscented wipes, as if a one-hour walk might blow up into a three-day camping trip in the wilderness due to circumstances that were frankly impossible to foresee. The summer sun drifted to noon in a hazy sky as Lucas tripped along the boardwalk, reaching his plump arms out toward the seagulls that strutted up and down and cased the ground with greedy eyes. "No sweetie, dirty!" Ellie cried, as he bent his little body down to tug at a piece of chewed gum.

"He should probably have lunch," Ellie said.

"Come Luke, come with Mama." She began unpacking her bag while I went to the concession stand and purchased the sort of lunch I remembered as a bit of heaven on a summer afternoon. How sublime it was to have a hot dog and fries under a clear blue sky as I knelt in the warm waves of sand. I would like that for Lucy, that pleasure. I supposed Ellie wouldn't approve. As soon as I rejoined them, Lucas fed his flax-bread sandwich to the dog and lobbied for my french fries by way of hurtling himself to the ground and pounding it with his fists.

I gave him one, and was surprised to observe that he used it as an implement for scooping ketchup out of the small paper cup I'd supplied. He stood very still, engrossed in his ritual: one swallow of ketchup. One swallow of sand. One inadvertent swallow of french fry shred. "All done, Mama."

I worried that Ellie would be mad at me, but she seemed to take it in stride, merely confining herself to pointing out the lesson. The only way children would eat nutritious food was a strict absence of alternatives. Broccoli or starvation. "A toddler's idea of a five-star restaurant would be a place that offers butter, relish, ketchup, and sand," she reflected. I laughed.

"I'll have the beurre blanc on tin foil, please."

"Very good, mademoiselle. Would you like to smear a sweet pickle jus reduction on your face with that?"

"No. Thank you. Just the butter, and maybe . . . what are your specials tonight?"

"Well, for soup we have a very good diaper rash cream or a swirl of water from the dog bowl. The pasta tonight is Kraft Dinner with strands of hair retrieved from inside a T-shirt. And the dessert is a choice of icing licked from a cupcake, or a cough drop found in the backyard."

"Thank you, I'll stick with the butter for now, and perhaps you could pour some apple juice down my pants."

Lucas upended the contents of my cardboard lunch tray on the boardwalk and then twined himself in Ellie's legs, his hair shining like sunlight. "You're so sleepy," she murmured to him, shifting the toddler onto her lap. She began to hum a lullaby and Lucas closed his eyes.

"You're very good at this, Ellie," I said. She snorted in protest and rocked the child softly.

"I'm hungry," I added. Ellie nudged her brimming bag of plenty toward me. "Help yourself."

The Ideal Husband

Calvin's Tuna Helper sulk was overdue, if truth be told. The tension had been building in him for weeks. He had been driving back and forth between Toronto and New York since midsummer, trying to honor his gigs with the Garden Snakes, and to otherwise hang on to life as he knew it: his customary pint of Double Diamond at the Ear; earning his rent by giving drum lessons; afternoons spent leafing through books on jazz history and comic book art at The Strand; and evenings on the phone, listening to me describe the plots of sad commercials. He sublet my apartment for me and carted up my favorite books and the few remaining clothes that fit, all strapped to the back of his Harley.

In his weeks and weekends in Toronto, he walked Kevin around Cabbagetown, stepping gingerly over the collapsed, snoring bodies of winos. He stoically adapted himself to David's décor aesthetic, mostly by confining himself to the basement, although there was one nightmarish episode when a friend persuaded him to drop acid for old time's sake, and he wound up lying under the glass coffee table in the deluded apprehension that he couldn't move, subjecting himself to every garish color and glinting figurine in Penny's living room for five hours, while the CD player skipped to the same place in a Fred Frith guitar solo. Over and over until his friend, who'd been outside marveling at dirt, came in and burst out laughing.

His nadir, however, was the weekend that he met my parents. It wasn't their fault. Nor his. Everyone was remarkably decent. The problem was the setting. The setting was a mistake. There are certain settings that fail to show everyone off to their best advantage, and here I would be thinking of a multivehicle road accident, for instance, or fetish night. But who knew that a windswept island in Georgian Bay would throw Calvin so profoundly off balance?

The meeting took place shortly after Calvin joined me in Toronto. We had driven up to Pointe au Barril in a rented Ford Taurus, playing Name That Tune, which turned into a hilarious Mexican standoff of mutual incomprehension.

When we arrived at the marina and he saw we would be taking a water taxi, he removed his fedora and ran his hands through his hair in distress.

"What's the matter?" I asked.

"Why do we have to go in a boat?"

"Because their cottage is on an island." I thought I had told him this already. I scanned the weathered marina buildings for the young Ojibway, Danny, who ran the taxi service.

"I don't do boats," Calvin announced.

"What are you talking about, you don't do boats? What does that mean?"

"I don't like them. I'm not going." He abruptly replaced his fedora and turned back toward the car, his feet in their ill-suited brogues slip-sliding on the uneven gravel.

"Calvin!" I stared in disbelief. "Where are you going?"

"Home." He was fumbling with the car rental key and slapping irritably at mosquitoes. I scurried after him and swung him by the shoulders to face me.

"What is this about? Are you that unnerved by meeting my parents?"

"No," he said, sounding definitive.

"Well then, what?" This was unforeseen. I'd never had a boyfriend who reared up whinnying at boats. "Is it some sort of environmentalist aversion? We don't have to take Danny's boat, we could borrow a canoe."

He cast his eyes away from me. I waited. Sweat trickled down between my breasts. It was stunningly humid. "I can't swim," Calvin finally said curtly.

"Oh," I said, raising my eyebrows, relieved and immeasurably surprised. "But you're a maritimer, I thought they all swam."

"Actually, no. Most of them don't. The Atlantic is too cold."

I thought about this. "Well, it isn't far, we just have to cross the bay. You can wear a life jacket."

"I'm not going to wear a life jacket," he said crossly. "I'll look like a four-year-old. I'd rather drown."

Danny pulled abreast of my parents' dock half an hour later, wiping sweat from his brow with his forearm. He killed the engine. The boat rose on the swell of its wake and banged against the dock's rubber bumpers. "Hoo hoo!" called my mother from farther up the hill. She and my father picked their way down between the blueberry bushes, across the rose-colored granite of the island, smiling and waving. Calvin was still huddled miserably in the boat, stuffed into an undersized life jacket that jutted up and out at the back like a jaunty orange cushion. He did, in fact, look four years old. His fedora, which had blown off his head en route and had to be rescued, was soaking wet. His hair stood up like tufts of grass.

Furious and cornered, he launched an outrageous preemptive strike.

"Hello," Calvin said to my parents. "I'm the guy who knocked up your daughter."

"Oh! Well . . ." my mother trailed off, flustered and trying to chuckle.

"Now, now," said my father, his smile frozen, as he rocked back and forth on the balls of his feet with his toes curling upward in tension.

"He's just joking," I said brightly. "Ha. Ha."

Danny hoisted our weekend bag onto the dock, and then he and I pushed Calvin out by his rear end so that he landed on the dock like a beached whale, facedown, well beyond humiliation and into some other plane of existence entirely. My parents gazed down at him nervously.

"I'm fine," he muttered into the dock, pushing up onto his hands and knees and finally standing with a wobble.

"Well, yes, of course," said my mother. "Don't be embarrassed, Calvin. All of Frances's boyfriends have been facedown on this dock at one time or another. Why don't you follow me?" She turned to lead him up the steep granite slope, but he couldn't get a purchase in his brogues and eventually had to half-crawl, half-crabwalk sideways. The ground evened out on a plateau covered thickly in pine needles, which proved just as slippery as the hill, so that Calvin fell on his knees twice en route to the weathered old cottage at the end of the path, on a promontory overlooking the restless waters of Lake Huron.

"Well, Calvin," said my father, when we were safely inside the cottage, "perhaps you'd like to borrow some shoes so that you don't have to crawl about the island all weekend long."

"No thank you," Calvin answered tersely, having collapsed into a white wicker chair. "I'll manage. I'll just go barefoot."

"Oh, I wouldn't do that," said my father. "There are rattlesnakes up here, you see, and loads of poison ivy."

"That's nice," Calvin said wanly. He threw up his hands. My father proceeded to outfit him in a pair of red cotton espadrilles with cork heels, which accented his black, stovepipe jeans like ballet slippers on a lumber-jack. I laughed. "You look like you could use a beer."

"Yes, I could."

There were some awkward moments after that, of course, particularly when I pushed my luck and insisted on playing a recording by the Garden Snakes, desperate to show off Calvin's strengths. We were sitting on the deck at sunset, my parents with their after-dinner coffees balanced on their knees, Calvin sipping his fourth or fifth beer. The evening was fragrant with pine and water, the atmosphere serene. Along came the blast of an atonal saxophone followed by the shriek of a rubber balloon. *Clang, crash, whine, bleat, blare.*

Calvin and my parents sat there absolutely frozen in a state of mutually polite acquiescence, as expressionless as it was possible to be without being dead.

"Maybe this isn't quite the right milieu," I offered. "It sounds really great in a bar." And my parents nodded their assurances that certainly it must, it was a very interesting, complicated sort of music, and Calvin was clearly very accomplished. "That squeaking sound," my father added uncertainly, "sounded rather like a dock bumper. What instrument would that be?"

"Balloon," Calvin said.

"Ah yes," said my father, nodding and curling up his toes.

I turned the music down until it was virtually inaudible, and busied myself making a smoothie.

"Care for a game of Scrabble?" my mother asked.

"I don't spell," said Calvin.

At that point, I gave up and went off to blunder through the brambles en route to the outhouse.

Let us assume, for argument's sake, that the man who sires your child is the man you are supposed to marry. He is the one man. Out of, let's say, one and a half billion grown men in the world, you get to have one. What do you want him to be like, this one man?

I always thought it might be nice if he were wealthy. " 'Bye, honey! Off I go to our ranch in Montana for a horseback trot and a Botox treatment. I'll meet you in the Caribbean villa. Don't forget to bring the maids."

Yet, a wealthy man might be driven, dictatorial, and sexist. He might be an appalling James Cameronish sort of man who flings televisions about in a temper. He would almost certainly have pathological issues. Who gets rich, if not men who are as insecure as gerbils at a roller derby?

So what if he just had a cushion of wealth, perhaps a little inheritance? Like the family cabin in Maine.

Too much to hope for? Could he have a steady income? Why, certainly not.

I do fantasize about an accomplished man. I've always dreamed of being part of a power couple, like Bill and Hillary Clinton. Only not. Alternatively, I could settle for being a clever and much-admired hostess, a muse, an invisible influence, married to someone like T. S. Eliot or Vincent Van Gogh. Insolvent, yes, but brilliant!

I wasn't really aiming for insolvent and pot-addled. But what about sex appeal? Surely there's that. A marriage with chemistry. Was it not the key to Bob the weight lifter? And Evan? These were gorgeous men, delicious men. I would have given up a lot, if truth be told, for the way they "grinned when they undressed." What a splendid history there is of such unions, after all. We may not be rich, we may not be accomplished, but we love passionately! We are Tristan and Isolde! We are Heathcliff and Cathy! We are Anna and Vronsky! We are me and this quite nice man I met, he's sort of quiet and his bum is oddly fan-shaped, but you'd like him.

We are me and a guy. Me 'n' him.

If you'll excuse me, I'm just going to go knock myself out with a bat.

"I could have married the president of France," I said to my mother the next morning, as I sat on the dock watching her don a severe white bathing cap and ease herself into the bay for a swim. "But inconveniently enough, I never met him."

"Calvin's a fine person," my mother replied, shoving off into a breast stroke.

"How do you know?"

"Because he loves you. You don't know what that means, Frances, but I do."

A Brief Note About the
Seventh Month of Pregnancy

You can't bend over to tie your shoes. It's the most surprising sort of handicap. Actually, you can't even see your shoes. You have to take it on faith that they match, that you are not wearing a sneaker on the right foot and a loafer on the left, and if you're pregnant in the winter, you simply cannot go outside unless you live with somebody who can zip up your boots, unless you wish to shuffle about like a deranged person and succumb to frostbite.

So there you are, in this baffling state of exile from your feet. Quite literally stopped in your tracks trying to peer over the hump of your belly. If you drop anything, like your house keys, you just have to stand there until an icicle forms on your nose waiting for someone to come home and let you in.

This leads me to a point about love. Being in love has

nothing to do with anything when you're seven months pregnant. You stop ruing your near miss with Michael Ignatieff, stop waxing nostalgic for ex-boyfriends and pining for Benicio Del Toro, and just thank God you've got anyone in a pair of pants standing beside you, simply to do up your shoes. Calvin became my home-care nurse around about October. He heave-hoed me out of bed; he helped me dress; he brought me hot-water bottles and Preparation H. He lent me his sweatpants and fed me his soup.

It's a different kind of love, this seven-months-pregnant love. It reveals itself slowly and only in retrospect. Looking back on it now, I cherish how tender he was. How patient and funny and fine.

A Man's Labor

Calvin and I went to our first prenatal class in November, something that I wouldn't recommend to other dating couples for a number of reasons, mostly having to do with the fact that Calvin passed out. Luckily, this happened a few hours later, after drinking nine mojitos at Julie's Bar—during which time he burst out with a number of proclamations related to planetary overpopulation and the environmental impact of diapers. I'm told this was inevitable. Prenatal classes, Ellie assured me, are the de rigeur method of making men face the fact that they're going to be fathers.

Here are a few things that you, as a woman, can engage in that will fail to get the Impending Infant notion across to men:

public episodes of vomiting

relocating to an entirely different country

shopping for snowsuits the size of a tea cozy

having sex wheelbarrow-style

You can ask them about this weird cognitive dissonance, and doubtless they'll offer that the experience of pregnancy is too mystifyingly feminine, like PMS and mascara. Therefore they don't embrace its implications. Au contraire, men warn one another away from womanly phenomena with such a superstitious reverence that they become stupid about the obvious. Even the sex is like: "Gee, honey, you seem to have developed elephantiasis in your midriff, but that's all right. I think I can just flip you over here, and . . ."

It doesn't register. You think they grasp it, but they don't. When I showed him my souvenir copy of the twenty-week ultrasound, Calvin examined it and said: "That's your baby? You're kidding. It looks like a map of Bosnia." Then he scanned it into David's computer and PhotoShopped a pope's hat onto the part of the image that apparently denoted the head. Ha, ha, ha, ha, ha, ha, ha . . .

Enter Mrs. Shenstone and her description of a man's role in labor. At that point reality wings across as decisively as a hockey puck to the forehead.

We arrived at Women's College Hospital after a languorous dinner of pork tenderloin and rosti at Episode, and took the elevator up to the fourth floor in the company of an orderly and his empty wheelchair, which I coveted for every single second of our ascent. Then we stepped out to find ourselves across from the maternity ward. You could hardly mistake it. The baby-blue doors were framed by a panorama of Winnie-the-Pooh posters, glued-on cherubs, and cardboard balloons featuring the names of newborn children. Happy relatives pushed through with their bouquets and baskets of food. A faint scent of roses wafted out across the hallway. Calvin froze, as if beholding the gates of Mordor.

"Is that where you're going to wind up?"

"I guess so."

He continued staring in horror. I was filled with my usual cocktail of pleasure and foreboding. On the one hand, the ward struck me as a cheerful female clubhouse which I had finally been invited to enter as a bona fide member. I unambiguously belonged somewhere, and that brought a certain relief.

On the other hand, *what the fuck have I done* and that sort of thing.

"Where's the class?" I looked around uncertainly. Down the pale green hall I spied another pregnant woman trudging like a pack mule with her stout husband shooing her along with one hand hovering at her back. We followed the pair into a bright classroom. Scallop-shaped plastic chairs had been arranged in a teardrop shape, with Mrs. Shenstone presiding at the pointy end, in front of a video machine. She had one leg crossed beneath her in a yoga position, with the other one dangling down to the white-tiled floor. She was wearing thick Guatemalan socks, riotously colored. They were pulled over black leggings, which in turn had been pulled over a magenta bodysuit, as if she were about to cartwheel into the splits. This was unlikely, given that she was sixty-four years old. Her ash-gray hair hung down to her waist like a worn-thin shawl. It also sprouted from her ears and furred her upper lip. She had one arm thrown over the back of her chair, and was grinning with the cocky, easy confidence of the one soldier in a room of recruits who had actually gone to war.

"Welcome," she called out in a robust voice, as I waddled to the far end of the teardrop. She watched in amusement as Calvin waved his arms about vaguely in an effort to help me sit down. "What are you doing?" I hissed. Then I saw that he was glancing at the other men, suddenly self-conscious about his capacity for chivalric gestures. One fellow was helping his sweet-faced wife peel a banana, as if her fingers were too weak. She cooed in appreciation. Another man, efficiently dressed for leisure in a crisp V-neck sweater and corduroy pants, was plumping a cushion for his spouse's chair, which he apparently had brought with him. A third, sporting sausage sideburns and square spectacles, was anxiously massaging his partner's thigh as she stretched out her legs and moaned conspicuously.

"Drama queen," I thought sourly. The more heavily pregnant I got, the more WASPish I became. Rectitude, for all my drunken face-plants of the last fifteen years, was apparently bred in my bones. Display no weakness, evince no emotion, and above all, reveal no connection to the flesh. Flesh is to be seen and not heard. Flesh is not to moan, simper, whine, or be audible in any way, and under no circumstances is flesh to involuntarily fart in public, as pregnant women are wont to do. Needless to say, this prohibition against physical demonstrativeness poses serious problems for the WASP experience of childbirth. What I dreaded about labor was the prospect of letting one rip while I pushed. And then pooping. Oh my God. Oh please, God, don't make me poop in front of Calvin.

The chairs gradually filled with huffing, puffing women and solicitous men, and everyone stared wildly all over the place to avoid one another's gaze. It was an awkward group encounter, insofar as the only thing we had in common was that we'd all fucked last March. You could argue that we were a small community of parents together, rather than a discomfited assortment of strangers with ravenous appetites and sore backs. You'd be right, but that's not how it felt. The transformation of consciousness is just one of the many miracles of childbirth. Something else entirely goes on in pregnancy. Mrs. Shenstone characterized it as the collective misery of being constipated with a bus.

"I'm here to tell you," she boomed, her pale blue eyes a-twinkle, "that you have never, ever experienced the kind of pain that you're all about to experience in six or seven weeks." She held up a peculiar object that turned out to be a woman's pelvis made of plush-toy material, hollowed out like a puppet for the purpose of demonstrating birth with your choice of African or Caucasian doll.

"Labor is not fun, it is not joyful. Those newfangled doulas and whatnot who run around proclaiming natural labor as some sort of religious experience are selling you a fantasy. Get rid of it." She flicked one hand imperiously. "Labor is wretched, my dears, that's the bad news. The good news is that it ends. I'm here to teach you how to get through it as comfortably and confidently as possible."

Calvin was looking alarmed. His eyes, I noted, were fixated on the plush pelvis, which Mrs. Shenstone was absentmindedly waving about. I myself was more fascinated by the chocolate-colored cloth doll on her table, which had a red-striped cloth twist for the umbilical cord. Now I could only imagine Miss Lucy that way, as brown and pliant and eyeless.

"In my day," Mrs. Shenstone continued, "we just passed out on an operating table, and woke up to our bundles of joy." Here she gave an unexpectedly high laugh, like a coyote yip. "Seven of them in my case, which is why I know of what I speak. If I could recommend that, I would. But obviously that kind of medication isn't good for you or your child, as we all learned, so we are going to find a middle road in this class. And we're going to talk about the men. I don't personally think there's much you can do in a delivery room but gape stupidly, but I'll give you a few suggestions. The main thing is that you know what your partner is going through. Sympathy is half the battle."

Calvin slumped in his chair. He clearly thought Mrs. Shenstone was on a worthless power trip at his expense.

What else he thought I didn't dare surmise. Mrs. Shenstone commanded that we announce our names and due dates. Shuffling feet and flitting smiles ensued, until one woman volunteered to pipe up and we were off. As each woman introduced herself, all the other women furtively checked her out. Belly size? Comparable? Bigger? Smaller? Like guys in a locker room shooting glances at each other's penises, we were trying to figure out— quickly, quickly—where we fit in the hierarchy of female fertility. One woman, the banana snacker who introduced herself shyly as Sheila, looked like she was pregnant with a newt. She just had this modest bump below her breasts, barely anything. She'd be the sort of teen mom you read about who blows through pregnancy without even noticing until she suddenly gives birth at an Arby's.

The woman with the perky, cushion-proffering husband turned out to be Stacy. She was a paragon of Sears catalog motherhood, in her pastel maternity tunic with matching leggings and cute tennis shoes. She rested her pretty, manicured hands on her perfectly round tummy and smiled very, very calmly. You could just tell she read *What to Expect When You're Expecting* over and over and over in a rocking chair in her baby's nursery and nothing floated through her head but yellow suns and pink booties and air.

Maureen, up next, was so pregnant that it was a wonder she hadn't been wheeled in on a trolley. The huge bulk of her womb lifted up her chic black skirt so high that it inadvertently became a mini, with two frightfully thin legs sticking out before disappearing at the other end into elegant black vinyl boots. I wondered what would happen if you knocked her onto her back. She would look rather like a beetle, waving her thin arms and legs about, with this frantic grimace on her face. The cell phone antenna jutting out over one ear at every "snack break" thereafter would complete the impression. Maureen was the executive assistant to the minister of finance, and about to give birth to twins, whom she intended to hand over at once to her husband, Albert, a chipper fellow, bald and bearded, who was finishing his Ph.D. in medieval tax law. (I asked him about his thesis when Maureen and I became friends, and I didn't understand a single word he said, except for *the* and *nobility*.)

The woman who was prone to moaning announced herself as Sirita. She was an actress, which possibly explained her absence of inhibition. She kept flipping her auburn curls out of her face and puffing and rubbing her legs beneath a flowing dress of scarlet wool. She was carrying low, like I was, revealing the dirty secret of never having done sit-ups in her life.

What the women thought of me, I wince to imagine, given that I sported hiking boots with mismatched laces, navy sweatpants that blatantly belonged to Calvin, and a leather jacket that couldn't be buttoned over my belly. It didn't matter what they thought; none of our jealous first impressions mattered. We were all part of the same club. At break time, we stampeded like a herd of wildebeests over to the snack table and devoured every dried apricot in sight.

PLAYING HOUSE

Later
9:30 P.M.
Julie's Bar on Dovercourt Road
The table in the bay window alcove

I drink ginger ale. Calvin Puddie drinks rum with soda, lime, and mint and makes the following points:

Point made during mojito number one.

"I am going to be with you during labor, Frannie, I am absolutely going to be there, but I'm telling you now that I'm not going to watch. I'll stand at your head and feed you ice chips or Valium or whatever, but that fucking plush-toy pelvis creeps me out and I'm not getting involved at that end."

Mojito 2.

"You realize that the world is overpopulated. I mean, in a way we have some nerve bringing a child into the world when there are five billion people in China alone. The kid is going to grow up and there won't be any food left. We'll bring somebody into the world and he'll have to scavenge for roots. I think we should have considered that."

Mojito 3.

"The other thing is the diapers. It's almost arrogant on our part to create that kind of environmental pollution just because we have a baby. Like, who do we think we are, having a baby?"

Mojito 4.

"I can't spend the next fucking year of my life putting diapers on a baby. I couldn't even put one on that ridiculous plastic doll without standing it on its head. There's just going to be shit everywhere. I'm going to wake up every morning and say, 'Hey, where's the shit? I need some on my T-shirt before I go out.' "

Mojito 5.

"I am a responsible man. I am a *modern* man. I am not going to run away just because you used the sponge for birth control, which is obviously about as effective as smearing marmalade in your vagina, and you got pregnant, so fine. I was just about to embark upon a career-defining recording session, but I canned it. I did. Because I'm a *good* man. But I'll tell you something right now. I am never, *ever*, going to sit cross-legged on the fucking floor to sing 'The Wheels on the Bus Go Round and Round.' I'm just not."

Mojito 6.

"You know what sucks? I'm gonna have a kid, and he's gonna make me go camping. I *hate* camping. I'm not taking him into the goddamn woods, ever, and I'm not taking him fishing. You want somebody who can do that, find another daddy. I will *gladly* waive my rights. *No problem.* I'm outta there. Had a kid, ruined my life, gave him up.

See ya later, you . . . you creature from the plushtoy-pelvis lagoon—

"Oh fug, I godda lie down."

Of Weaver Birds and Women

Calvin slept in the next morning, and so did I. Of course I did. My vocation in life now was to sleep. I would edit perhaps two sentences of a magazine story assigned to me, or Marina's one-woman play, fix a comma and some spelling, and then find it necessary to have a three-hour nap. Just snoozin' away like a hibernating bear, dreaming that I'd given birth, but that the baby fell off the hospital bed and rolled underneath it and we couldn't find her. We looked and looked. Or dreaming that the baby was only one inch long, so that my nipple was bigger than its head and I couldn't breastfeed and gave it to the Humane Society.

Dreaming that the baby turned out to be Michael Ignatieff, the damnedest thing, and I hadn't given birth in the hospital after all, but in Coney Island, and had nothing to feed him but corn dogs.

I sent Ignatieff's article back to Gill, the managing editor at *The Pithy Review,* and allowed that I could not edit it, now, for my brain was a slosh of sentimentality and fatigue. I had lost my capacity for abstract thought and tended to spend hours doodling in the margins of the manuscript and weeping over its contents. "I'm pregnant, Gill, that's the trouble."

"Oh my God! That is so great!" she yelled, and her unabashed joy was so unexpected that it warmed me all day. She appointed me editor-at-large, which was fitting on several levels, and I let it go. For now. I let it go because I was tired of making decisions. I wanted to crawl in to the clubhouse and curl up and relax in the knowledge that my task was unassailable. Having a baby? Come on in. The invitation is unqualified.

Every now and then, I emerged from hibernation to dutifully tend my brother's house.

"What are you doing?" Calvin asked, watching me from the patio door one morning.

"I'm cutting the lawn."

"With scissors?"

"Well, I couldn't find anything else."

"Like what couldn't you find? A saw? Nail clippers? Did you look for the lawn mower, by any chance?"

"Yes I did." I stood up to look at him, rubbing the small of my back. "I couldn't find one."

He sighed and disappeared into the garage to get the lawn mower. "Out of the garden," he ordered upon reemerging. "You're fired."

One night, unable to sleep because I weighed one

thousand pounds and had to keep shifting lest various limbs went numb, it hit me powerfully that what I really wanted to do was "nest." According to Dr. William Sears in *The Baby Book*, under the heading "Preparing Your Nest," all pregnant women wish to redecorate houses. Because they have tummies, and they are weaver birds. "You've glanced wishfully through those baby magazines for months," Sears writes, all-knowingly, "admiring the dazzling colors of designer nurseries, the animal-appliquéd bedding and matching ensembles. Now, with birth only weeks away, you too can design your nest and outfit your baby as plain or as fancy as your imagination and your budget allow."

Not so. This was absolutely verboten in David's house, although the notion gnawed at me and persisted, and I began to move little things about, just here and there, snatching the odd figurine from the living room and hiding it in the basement, for example, or placing framed photos of Penny and David facedown as I waddled through various rooms. At the same time I began to shop, in a similarly furtive and piecemeal fashion.

I arrived home one day with ten receiving blankets and slid them into Penny's linen closet. Another day I came home with a box of teensy terrycloth sleepers and salted them away in various drawers. At one point my nesting instinct took an apocalyptic turn and I developed an overwhelming need to go Y2K shopping.

I had worried about Y2K, you know, and then I hadn't anymore, and then I had, and then hadn't, and then I tried to catch up on who was compliant, and gotten confused, and then decided, well, I'd better do a little shopping just in case. But I couldn't determine what to buy. The peril was unclear. Nothing could happen, or civilization could end. Working within those parameters, I went to a hiking outfitters store and got a flashlight. Then I stared for a long time at the freeze-dried food, featuring organic black bean hummus for $8.95. I wondered if that wasn't a bit precious, for surviving the end of the world. You'd probably shoot your neighbor for their Spam if conditions reached the point where freeze-dried food supplies were necessary.

"Listen to this Gallup Poll," I told Calvin, waving the *Toronto Star* at him in the kitchen one morning, "only seven percent of Canadians 'expect their personal lives to be disrupted in a major way.' Yet thirty-five percent 'expect shortages of food.' "

"Just not their food," Calvin said. "Someone else's food will be disrupted."

My mother advised me to buy diapers. Ellie urged the purchase of vitamins. My father quoted Eugene Weber on theories of apocalypse. Annabelle phoned from B.C.: "You can't know," she said. "You cannot know from this end of things that motherhood is the hardest job you're going to have."

Indecisive and anxious and behaving like a weaver bird, I came and went each day and eventually filled my brother's house up with so many random objects that his carefully appointed castle began to resemble a Dollar Store.

Confinement:
1. the act or an instance of confining; the state of being confined.
2. the time of a woman's giving birth.

The interesting thing about babies, I've found, is that even if you do not wish to give birth to them—even if you adamantly do not wish to because it has lately occurred to you that they will move into your house and not leave for twenty years, whereas before you were somehow thinking that they would be visiting just briefly—even though you feel that way, they know how to make you cry uncle. What they do is they turn your tummy into a special effects bonanza out of a David Cronenberg movie. And this begins to freak you out. You lie in the bath, for example, and you watch this huge, taut mound where your stomach used to be assuming a variety of shapes, while the creature beneath the skin moves restlessly about like an animal under a carpet.

"I don't want this anymore," I told Calvin. "I'm going

to explode like that guy in *Monty Python and the Meaning of Life.*"

He was sitting on the toilet, waiting dutifully to hoist me out of the tub. "She'll come out when she's ready," he said, echoing what we'd learned in prenatal class.

"How can she not be ready? She doesn't fit anymore. Her toes must be up her nose."

"We could try going for a walk," he offered. I got dressed, Calvin tied my boot laces and eased on my shearling coat, and I hobbled out into the icy dark of December on Carleton Street, immediately slipping on the stairs of my brother's house and tobogganing down them on my ass.

"That should help," Calvin said.

It did not. He escorted me to Riverdale Park and we walked around and around in the shadows, our breath puffing out in little clouds, past the snowy cemetery, past the silent petting zoo, past the Victorian houses with their Christmas wreaths and icicle lights, under the barren elms and maple trees. Kevin trotted ahead of us, poking his nose into frozen bits of poop. Round and round we went, without speaking, almost falling into a trance, and everything we knew about ourselves fell away, spinning off like drops of water in the centrifugal force of the circle we tread, and we were suspended in this moment of not knowing, of simply waiting for our lives to begin.

At midnight, my midriff began to tighten. I opened my eyes, looked at the clock, and said, "No, absolutely not. I'm too tired." The next day, the squeezing sensation intensified while we were watching *The Poseidon Adventure* on video, and all the passengers were plummeting from the upside-down chandelier in the ballroom. I grunted.

"What was that?" asked Calvin.

"Nothing," I said.

I grunted again.

"Why are you making that sound?"

"No reason."

Please, God, stop making me sound like that.

"You just did it again."

"Well, I'm sorry."

"Doesn't Shelley Winters drown in this scene? When she tries to swim all the way underwater?"

"I don't remember."

(Shelley Winters: "Don't argue, Mr. Scott. I was the underwater swimming champ of New York three years running when I was seventeen.")

"That's cool, she was seventeen for three years."

"Oh shit, oh shit. Calvin, I think my water just broke!"

"Right. Shit." He leapt from the couch and stared, aghast, as I gushed all over my brother's zebra carpet. "Quick," he shouted, "quick." He ran off to find me a clean pair of sweatpants, tossed them at me and then sort of hopped about uncertainly for a while before remembering that one thing he might do was call a cab.

It was raining outside. We stood on my brother's steps waiting for Diamond Taxi and watching cars creep nervously by on Carlton Street, losing their purchase on the slick, quickly freezing surface of the asphalt. I grunted. Calvin kept looking nervously at his watch, as if the future Miss Mackenzie had made an appointment. And then he just aimlessly fretted. "Ah, fuck this, this is ridiculous, could we have picked worse weather for a swift trip to the hospital? How about a sandstorm? I know, let's move to Bermuda and go into labor just as gale-force winds from Hurricane Abdul hit the coast. Or I have a better idea. Let's hike into the Himalayas and give birth in an avalanche. Or better yet, why don't we move to Toronto and wait for a cab in the freezing rain?"

I grunted.

A taxi appeared about half an hour later, driven by a glaring, mustachioed man wearing a furuq. He waited impatiently for us to reach him across the barely naviga-ble garden, eyeing us disdainfully as we slid around like hogs on ice and finally tugged on his door handle.

Calvin stuffed me in and ran carefully around the car to get in the other door. "Women's College Hospital," he told the driver.

"What is she doing?" the man asked Calvin, watching me in his rearview. "Is she in her time?"

"We're just going to the hospital, that's all."

"Because I do not want a birth in my car, I'm not trained."

"We're going ten blocks," Calvin reminded him. "You'll be fine."

We inched along, gently careering this way and that, and then almost rear-ended a malfunctioning streetcar. "Don't worry," the driver said. "The conditions are much worse in Kabul. At least you have good roads. In Kabul, rain like this, forget it. You leave the car and walk."

"When did you come here from Afghanistan?" Calvin asked, polite.

"Ten years. Since before Taliban. People here think they are mad, but before them it was just as crazy. The Russians." He shook his head.

I concentrated on my positive thinking exercises. I am not being squeezed to death by a boa constrictor, I am being hugged by Barney. Big hug. Another big hug. Why, yet another big hug.

"Calvin," I hissed, "tell him *to stop driving this fucking car,* it's making me crazy."

We had been lurching forward, bit by bit, and every subtle jolt exacerbated the contractions. Within a block of the hospital, I couldn't stand it anymore and burst out of the taxi, slip-sliding the rest of the way there with Calvin running and falling and running to catch up with me after paying off the driver.

The labor nurses settled us into a large, dark, windowless room featuring a wide array of medical equipment. After a cursory examination, Betty, a tall, lively woman from the Dominican Republic sporting scrubs and green gardening clogs, who was the doctor on call that afternoon, advised us that I was four centimeters dilated.

"You have a way to go," she said, "so just relax, focus on your breathing, and let us know when you think you want pain medication."

I did want pain medication, but I didn't want to give in this early in the whole affair. You aren't supposed to want it so soon, you're supposed to feel the pain, breeeeathe through it, throooough the pain. Why? Because then you can feeeeel the pain. I threw up. I buckled over. I staggered in circles. This was it, I realized, my life on the crest of a wave, I cried my eyes out, mourning everything over my shoulder receding behind me.

Calvin had brought a little ghetto blaster and popped in a Van Morrison tape. "Isn't that nice music? Nice and relaxing? It's a marvelous night for a moon dance." Breathe throooough the pain, throoough the pain.

"Calvin, turn that bloody music off!"

The labor nurse poked her head into the room. "How about a shower, honey? Warm water helps. It's just around the corner to the left."

Calvin escorted me to the shower room and I climbed glumly into the narrow stall. The water had about as much effect on my pain as ant breath. My body was a violent, supercell storm. I just wanted to escape, climb out of my body and disappear through some window, get away from the frantic harassment of pain.

"Make it stop!" I howled.

Calvin reached in hastily and turned off the shower.

"Not the shower, Calvin, the pain."

He turned the shower back on. I grunted and gnashed my teeth and vomited down into the swirling drain. *"Oh, God, make it stop."* Calvin obediently twisted the faucet again.

"Oh for God's sake, Calvin, get a clue."

At this he ran off to find the nurse, who paged the anaesthesiologist, who arrived some time later with his creepy epidural kit in tow. I flinched as the needle sank into my back, and then a tingling chill flew up my spine. Presently a becalming sense of numbness settled into my neck, chest and arms. My stomach, however, remained a roiling nightmare. "Calvin," I ventured, between gasps, "I think he froze me from the waist up." At this he ran to find the nurse, who paged the anaesthesiologist, who returned with the obstetrician on call, two residents, and an intern.

They gathered around me murmuring in fascinated surprise, as if discovering a beached sea monster.

"Well, for heaven's sake," said the anaesthesiologist. "I've never seen this before."

"Did you enter the puncture in lumbar two?" wondered the obstetrician.

"I believe so. But somehow the nerves clearly—"

"Excuse me," bellowed Calvin. They all looked up in startlement. He was wild with anxiety, his T-shirt drenched with sweat, his face unshaven, his hair a swirl of cowlicks. "Could you fix this, because I think it's safe to say that your patient is *still in pain.*"

"Oh yes, of course."

They got the point and turned their attention and their instruments to me. But it was too late. I needed to push and I found, to my sobbing amazement, that I couldn't stop pushing, that my lower body was heaving and shuddering and squeezing, engrossed in its primitive mission with no heed to my mind, which was helpless, suspended, stranded there above my frozen heart. I could scream all I wanted, bite Calvin's hand, bellow hoarsely, snarl, weep. No matter. My child pulled me into my life.

"It's a boy!" someone in the large, assorted crew of medical professionals shouted cheerfully.

A boy. Not me, multiplied. But someone brand-new. He let out a small, surprised cry as the nurses jostled him along from my body to their blanketed scales, and then Calvin had him, his son in his arms, and he was mesmerized, grinning, he wouldn't let him go. He brought him to me, holding him for us both for my arms were still frozen, and the baby gazed blinkingly up at my face.

"Hello, lemon," I said. I don't know why. Arbitrary words for a love as certain and clear and sweet as sunlight. Hello peach, hello honey, hello stranger, hello you.

How We Come Alive

This was a time of wonder. Calvin and I rarely spoke, or at least not in English. I communicated in jagged sobs and jabbered coos, our baby expressed himself in hoarse little mewls, and Calvin sang. I could hear him singing just under his breath, snatches of what sounded like "Lush Life" into a tiny ear. He took to scooping the baby up and departing, just leaving the room for stretches of time, exploring the halls, simply feeling the weight of his son.

When I could—when the baby was safe in his father's arms and I was able—I walked out of the hospital in sweatpants and overcoat, and shuffled along Bay Street taking exercise in the unfamiliar daylight.

Daylight! How do you do? Not even very nice daylight, dishwater gray and glumly cold. But I hadn't seen the outside since Before. And now was another time, an afterward as distinct, I am certain, as anything I will ever know.

We come to see that life divides at this threshold, that when we walk along the beach ever after, where the waves sprawl upward in spidery undulations to wash the shore, we will reach down with the driftwood we've idly gathered and write, not our own name, but our child's. We do come to know that, and to inhabit our larger selves with a deepened sense of patience and grace, but the transformation is blinding for a while, the way we shut our eyes tight when we fall.

After a few blocks, I reached a bench and sat down, staring around me at the understood points of light, the Christmas bulbs twinkling red and green in shop windows as they did when I lived in New York and passed them on my way through bitter canyon winds to work; as they did when I was a student freed up by exams, walking happily to the Morrisey Tavern on Yonge Street to party with a pitcher of beer; as they did when I stood before them reverently, as a child.

Now I looked at them in the windows of the Shopper's Drug Mart in downtown Toronto and felt myself fixed in this epiphany, this changed self that was nothing, yet, but an inchoate muttering on the sidewall:

"I have a son."

A man, a woman, a child. A trio of strangers. Three pieces of a puzzle whose pattern of connection are fixed, but not revealed. We stared at the child, me and Calvin in our pale-green hospital room, and thought: *Hmmmm . . . and you are . . . ?*

We strain to see our likenesses in his face, and then

our mutual implicit query is the same: ". . . and you are . . . ?"

You: Frances Mackenzie?

You: Calvin Puddie? You are . . . ?

We had very few clues. Our baby weighed eight pounds. We hoped that this would be the only time in his life when poundage was his most distinctive trait. His hair was a dark and sweet-smelling fuzz that the nurses assured us meant nothing. His eyes were puffy, his gaze was vague, his fingers were finely tapered. His personality alternated between coma and squall. He was ripe for projection.

"He's the spitting image of Calvin," said my mother, who had arrived late for the birth with a cell phone glued to her ear, trying to talk a patient out of suicide.

"He is *not* the spitting image of Calvin," I objected. "There isn't even the remotest resemblance."

"Well now, I think he has my sister's face," said my father, as he tilted gingerly toward his grandson from across the hospital room. "Certainly, I remember that from her baby pictures."

"He's a peach," said the nurse. "He looks like his mum."

"I just don't know how you can tell that," said Calvin, studying the baby's face.

"Don't you see a resemblance to anyone?" I asked.

"No. Do you?"

"No."

But we shared him, we knew that much, because we both loved him with a tenderness so exquisite and complete that it moved us to wondering stillness.

The Modern Christening

"Well now, Freddie, what are you going to name the little fellow?" my father asked, returning to this quandary
of identity in short order. We were crowded into Penny
and David's bedroom now. My mother wore a celebratory sort of outfit, which took the form of a scoop-necked
white blouse and frilled black skirt, as if she'd just given
an organ recital; my boyfriend sported a spit-up bib
neatly flanking each shoulder on his circa '50s bowling
shirt; my anxious father milled about the room in his
tweed hat, still a-sparkle with melting snowflakes; and
our confused, adopted dog kept peering up at everyone
and tentatively wagging his tail.

The master bedroom, with its plump mattress beneath
silver satin sheets, silk-fringed antique lampshades, and
sleek armless chairs, had become the baby's nursery, de-
spite frantic admonitions to the contrary from David,

who was stranded in England by Penny's holiday party plans. He was in no position to defend his boudoir from the sinister inward drift of Huggies coupons, and I was in no position to think. The basement was too cramped, that was all, and the guest room was neck-high in chick-peas and other peculiar supplies.

My father held his cross-eyed, dark-haired, snuffling grandson in the inimitable manner of Men of an Older Generation, which is to say, as if he were handling something razor-sharp, or covered in quills. He persisted with his inquiry. "You know, it's been five days and he remains anonymous. I'd like to address him as young So-and-So."

It gnawed at him, this namelessness, as if he were unable to accept his new identity as a grandfather until we'd fixed it. What was the name? Did he, or did he not, descend in a discernable line from the ancestral Macken-zies of Inverness?

"His name is Gim," Calvin announced, reclaiming the baby from my father and settling him carefully into his lap as he lowered himself onto the settee. The baby startled, throwing up his arms in surrender and then gradually allowing them to relax.

"No it's not," I blurted out, my red-rimmed eyes widening in indignation. "You can't just decide that. He can't be called Gim."

Calvin studied me with steely resolve. "Gim Knutson, my musical mentor. Gim Puddie-Mackenzie, my pro-tégé."

"Gim has nothing to do with anything!" I said, bursting into tears, which happens to sleep-deprived people roughly every half hour. Not tears of sentiment, as in pregnancy. But wild, aggressive, irritable sobs touched off by modest predicaments, like a forecast of "light snow."

"How dare you? That's like naming him Vishnu, it has nothing to do with who we are."

"Oh, really?" Calvin challenged, jutting out his unshaven chin. "And who are we? Our ancestors have nothing in common. You're a WASP, I'm a working-class Acadian. I don't think you have a clue how far apart that sets our ancestry. You've never even met my family, so how do you know I don't have an Uncle Vishnu?"

"Of course you don't have an Uncle-fucking-Vishnu. Who would name somebody Vishnu Puddie?"

"A few months ago," Calvin continued, "I was a musician. That's my tradition, and that's my lineage."

"But Calvin, Gim sounds ridiculous. How can you do this to me?"

"Calvin is making a valid point," my mother interjected. "Lineage doesn't have to be directly familial, it can be cultural, or occupational. The baby doesn't have to be connected explicitly, per se, to an ancestry of coal-mining Puddies."

"Oh, get out," I wailed at my mother. "That's so unmaternal of you to take his side."

"Now Calvin," ventured my father, gamely suppressing his panic, "I fully understand your desire for cultural lineage, but perhaps there's a more melodious name, a more—"

"All right: Buster," Calvin countered. "Buster or Gim, those are your choices."

"Why are you doing this to me?" I screamed, causing my son to awaken and cry.

Calvin stood up and placed the baby tenderly against his chest, rocking back and forth. "I'm not *doing* anything to you. I'm just trying to impose a little of myself on my progeny. Is that so threatening? This has been all about you. Your pregnancy, your parents, your anxieties, your"—he waved his hand about to indicate the room—"this preposterous house. You drag me out of my life, you wear my clothes, you cry on my shoulder, you make fun of me if I want to watch hockey on TV—"

"What?"

"So *my son* is either going to be named Buster or Gim."

"I never made fun of you for wanting to watch hockey."

"Yes, you did."

My parents, who had been rooted to their spots, elected, at this point, to tiptoe out of the room.

"Go ahead," I muttered, my rage rendered aimless by my fatigue. "Watch hockey. I didn't realize it made you so self-conscious."

"Well, I am self-conscious," he said defensively, "because I don't know who I'm supposed to be. I don't know who I am to you, and I don't know who I am to me." As he said this, he danced slowly in a circle with the baby, who was pressing his face sleepily into his father's sweater and taking shivery breaths, his fingers kneading the wool. It occurred to me that whether or not Calvin ever said it out loud, or even consciously discovered it, he knew exactly who he was to his child.

"Lester," he muttered, some hours later in the darkness beside me, buried deep beneath Penny's down comforter.

"What did you say?"

"Lester," he repeated. "Like Lester Bowie. That's my final offer."

I Envy Calvin's Penis, Dr. Freud. Why Doesn't He Envy My Sleep Deprivation and Hemorrhoids?

They say that men are envious of women for giving birth, that that is why they strive so hard in war and commerce, why they rage and clash swords and build palaces of marble, why they compose operas, why they rape—because they are driven to overcome their helpless sense of exile from the one singular triumph that is motherhood.

I can't really say I picked up that vibe from Calvin. In the dark afternoons of later December 1999, he reclined in various corners of my brother's house as carefully and quietly as a man who has fallen through a space-time hole and landed on an unidentified planet, cautious about making any sudden movements lest he aggravate the aliens. The sleep-deprived vitriol I hurled at him at all hours was partly to blame, and it dated from the very first days of the baby's life—which, if I may just say so, is largely the fault of the modern maternity ward. If you are weary and in need of rest, because, for example, you have just spent forty-five hours vomiting in a shower stall, I wish to point out that you will not recover smoothly on the modern maternity ward. Sleeping, I discovered, is a highly frowned-upon activity. Brand-new mothers may well be the most exhausted group of human beings this side of infantry troops, but they are not allowed to sleep on a maternity ward because sleeping is inconvenient to nurses. Nurses are not sleepy. No. They are zippy and energetic. They are energized by their mysterious hostility to new mothers, therefore they find it necessary to blow in and out of rooms like waiters in a saloon, and they are all very zippy and energetic, and you are not, and they don't care.

They barge in to check your pulse, change your sanitary napkin, hand you forms, make you drink ice water, poke you in the stomach, measure your temperature, remove the IV from your hand, make you eat pork chops, ask if you want to have a photograph taken with your newborn, remove the newborn (who has been wrapped in a green table napkin and resembles a pupa) to have his foot pricked, then wheel him back in, newly bawling, and ask in a cheerful bellow if you're ready for the breast-feeding seminar down the hall.

No, I am not. My body has been hit by an asteroid so would you all just kindly fuck right off.

No we won't. We won't fuck right off. The walls may be covered in pretty posters of Winnie-the-Pooh and Bambi, but we are the legions of Satan.

"Sit up, Mrs. Mackenzie, it's time to change your sheets."

"Huh? What?" This would have been on day two, before my escape to David's. I lifted my leaden head and gazed around, uncomprehending; I had now had roughly three minutes' sleep since the day before I started watching *The Poseidon Adventure*. After an interlude of elation, where sing-songed announcements were made by hospital phone to Marina and Ellie and my sister and two ex-boyfriends and the guy I went to grade school with in Ottawa and my professor at Columbia and some woman I met, once, on a plane, all I wanted to do was phone 911.

"Emergency, how may I direct your call?"

"I need to have a nap."

"Are you alone at this time in a comfortable bed with your nightie on?"

"Nurses are breaking into my room and I don't know what to do."

I slipped out of my two-inch-wide hospital bed and limped to the beige vinyl chair that held my overnight bag and shoved it against the door, thus rather feebly barricading myself in. What I desired was my son and unconsciousness, both. I wanted to draw him into me, back into me, not hidden or abstracted but like a lover this time, the tiny, sweet-smelling love of my life, enfolded in my body with our breath mingling and our silence and vulnerability shared. I lifted him out of his Plexiglas bassinet and tucked him in beside me, my chin on his hot little head, his cheek against my neck, and at last, for a handful of hours, we slept.

Calvin, by contrast, had gone home after the baby was

born and snoozed for ten hours like a big fat hog. No nurses, no baby, just darkness and limitless quiet. For this reason, I now felt compelled to despise him. Here came a raging source of relationship conflict, entirely uncharted.

"You evil, evil sleep hog!" I snapped at him, when the father of my child walked in with flowers and bagels in the wan morning sunlight. "How dare you abandon me in this ostensible hospital which is actually a Taco Bell and go home and sleep?"

It was disorienting for him, needless to say, to encounter a vision of Linda Blair from *The Exorcist* when he was expecting something more akin to a painting by Mary Cassatt—a plumply serene mother with her soft breast exposed to a beaming child. I tried, I really did; I wanted to conform to that image of maternal bliss, but it was tricky. Every time I opened my mouth to say, "Calvin, aren't we blessed?" what came out instead was something roughly along the lines of: *"Your mother sucks cocks in hell"* in a slurred, demonic voice, as my head spun around and I spat lime-green bile. Then I'd clap my hand to my face and mutter, "Oh dear, I'm so sorry."

And ten minutes later, do it again.

I longed to be one of Mary Cassatt's watercolor mamas, so relaxed and composed, for men would admire a woman like that, you could tell. I was therefore struggling to stop being a woman like me, who was simultaneously incontinent in the bladder and constipated in the bowel, limping around flabbily, hunting for the Preparation H, and otherwise inadvertently squirting jets of milk at the wall and into the toaster and all over her jumbo-sized bathrobe.

Calvin ducked my shrieks and stared studiously beyond my physical dishevelment, sucking up his own violent emotions until he was so filled with them that he was as stiff and jerky as a man who'd swallowed cement. He teetered around the house as if he couldn't bend at the knees, muttering "No problem," and "I'll get you some juice right away," going *clomp, clomp, clomp* in his cement feet. He had, at any rate, absolutely nothing to offer on the subjects of child rearing, motherhood, and breast-feeding, and ran for the door—stiffly, jerkily—when the feminine hordes arrived with their outbursts of excited advice.

In truth, I would have followed him out the door if I could have. Given that human beings have managed to exist for several million years, I naively assumed that breast-feeding an infant was a simple matter of sticking your breast in its mouth. I did not realize that breast-feeding required the expert intervention of six books, seventeen relatives, and the La Leche League. Indeed, the only conclusion to be drawn from the fact that breast-feeding cannot be accomplished without vigorous instruction by trained professionals is that all human beings who survived infancy prior to the twentieth century did so by fluke. Alternatively, natural selection dictated that all mothers who allowed themselves to be lectured by a large group of other women ensured the survival of their genes, whereas mothers who breast-fed their infants on their own and failed to master the "football hold" promptly ended their lineage. Therefore, human beings evolved into social creatures capable of refined consultation leading to the dawn of civilization because of their inability to feed newborn humans without an instructional video.

Or Mae Givens, who frightened Calvin so badly that you'd have thought she was an apparition when she banged on our door.

Mae Givens was a stout woman with rough-cropped gray hair tapering into sideburns, dark eyebrows jumping up over her unrimmed glasses, and a long, rather aquiline nose. She showed up one morning after I apparently had consented to a visit from the La Leche League in my maternity-ward delirium. In the ensuing days, as my breasts hardened into volleyballs, I forgot all about the La Leche League and was duly following the directions of the marauding nurses and their pamphlets, with additional instruction from my sister via telephone and a video I'd been given at prenatal class.

The La Leche League had not forgotten, for they had a missionary zeal about breast-feeding and had earmarked me as a convertible savage.

Mae Givens wore a paisley cotton shawl wrapped high around her neck like a fringed bandage. As she removed her brown wool coat I noticed that she smelled faintly of patchouli. I found it interesting—that almost mystical connection between lactation consulting and 1970s commune values. But I worried that it would offend Mae if I just brought it up right out of the blue. So I sat dumbly on Penny's bed and just offered my breasts for inspection.

Lester was asleep in his wicker basket, and my nipples

were dripping, the warm sticky milk running through my fingers and snaking down my flabby midriff. I hated that feeling of leaking fluid from every orifice, as if I literally couldn't contain myself, and the presence of this stranger made it worse.

"Oh, don't worry," said Mae, handing me a cloth. "Your flow will adjust as you and Baby get into your own rhythm."

"And when will that be?"

"Usually six months. It flies by." She sat down in Penny's overstuffed armchair and pushed up the sleeves of her sweater. "For the final four years that I nursed Callum? It was totally on demand. My breasts knew exactly when he would want num-nums." She gave out an odd little hoot of laughter.

"You breast-fed for more than four years?" I wasn't sure I'd heard her correctly.

"I did, yes." She nodded emphatically, blinking her owlish eyes. "I certainly did. I mean, that's what primates do. They allow the baby to wean himself when he's ready. I think it's what all women are meant to do, although I understand that some are made to feel too ashamed by their husbands."

I must admit that it had never occurred to me to breast-feed Lester for longer than I could stand going without a martini, which I was playing by ear. The thought of a child actually old enough to call my breasts "num-nums" was extremely disconcerting.

"Why is it important to be like a primate?" I wondered.

165

"Well, you know, many of our essential behaviors are reflected in our closest cousins in nature. Patriarchy has taught us to reserve our breasts for men, but that is not what nature tells us."

Nature has no authority on the subject, given that it didn't supply us with automatic breast-feeding expertise. "Didn't you want your breasts back, Mae? You know for, for"— *for what?*—"to just reserve them for you and your bra?"

"Toward the end," Mae confided, crossing her legs and rubbing what appeared to be a touch of eczema on her hand, "I was convinced that I was the only woman in the world nursing a five-year-old! But I loved it. I thought I was a pioneer, blazing out new territory. Then I found Kathy Dettwyler's books—I don't know if you've read her . . ." I shook my head and clutched at the bedspread. "Well, she says it's normal for a child to nurse for seven years, so I was very relieved to hear that. Dr. Dettwyler really saved my self-image."

I settled back on my pillows and ran my tongue against the inside of my cheek, trying to recall my sister's kids at the age of five, how they already knew who the Spice Girls were, how they asked emphatic questions about their genitals and dressed up endlessly as brides and princesses and superheroes. I imagined my nephew Eric in his Spiderman costume bursting into Annabelle's room and then bouncing onto the bed to shove up her sweater. Oh, no, no, no. That just didn't play right. I shooed the image out of my head.

"How did this breast-feeding come to an end?" I

asked. Mae cocked her head, trying to remember, a pleased smile playing on her lips.

"Sometime around the time Callum turned five, he started sleeping through the night."

My eyes widened. He started sleeping through the night when he was *five?*

"So that's when I weaned him. Okay, how long has it been since Baby's last feed?" she asked, signing off on our personal chat and getting down to business. I didn't like that word, *feed,* like I was an ambulatory swine trough. Time for Baby's Feed from the Breast. I began to feel uncooperative.

"I don't know," I shrugged. "I forget."

"Okay, well, he shouldn't be going longer than two hours at this point so we'll just give him a little tickle here . . ." She jabbed at Lester's face. He rubbed his nose back and forth against his sheet and began to whimper.

"There we are," cooed Mae, collecting him from the basket. "Now let me see how you hold him. No, that's not going to help Baby get his job done. You have to position Baby close to you, with his hips flexed, so that he doesn't have to turn his head to reach your breast. His mouth and nose should be facing your nipple."

Inconveniently, my nipple was on the underside of my breast, so Lester essentially had to be inserted underneath and backward, which is not in your average La Leche League positioning manual. Mae was a bit stymied.

"Let's try the cross-cradle position with the U hold." She began folding me and Lester like origami.

"Okay, Fran, place your fingers flat on your ribcage

under your breast with your index finger in the crease under your breast. Drop your elbow so that your breast is supported between your thumb and index finger . . ." She reached for my breast and bunched it in her hand like bread dough.

"You support Baby with the fingers of your right hand, do you see? Do it by gently placing your hand behind his ears and neck with your thumb and index finger behind each ear . . . no, that looks like you're going to strangle him. The palm of your hand is placed between his shoulder blades. When Baby opens his mouth wide, you push with the palm of your hand from between the shoulder blades. His mouth will be covering at least a half inch from the base of your nipple."

Oh, aaarrrgh. I wanted to hit her over the head with a pan. It was like trying to follow Ikea furniture directions.

"Don't worry," said Mae. "You'll get the hang of it. The worst thing is to give up. You must never give up. Don't let them persuade you to quit. Their arguments will sound very seductive, you know, and you just have to remember your baby." As if in reply, my unused left breast, which Mae was still clutching, suddenly shot a stream of milk at her face like a prank corsage.

"Oh, I'm so sorry," I stammered. She gave out another little hoot.

"Let's try the football position, which helps when a mother has a forceful milk ejection reflex. In the football position you support Baby's head in your hand and his back along your arm beside you and support your breast with a C hold . . ."

To complete your assembly of the Noot bookshelf, fold tab G here and insert peg 567$%B.

"The important thing," said Mae, "is to be sure he's actually drinking and not just sucking. When he begins to receive milk, you will see his jaw working all the way back to his ear. His temples will wiggle. You will also hear him swallowing, quickly at first, then more slowly, as his appetite is satisfied."

We both gazed at Lester expectantly. He seemed to be doing just exactly what he wanted to be doing, quick little sucks and then a pause, as he drifted on waves of sleep, then more little sucks. Calm and unruffled and sweet.

Holy Cow

Ellie was another model of motherhood, although I couldn't quite piece together which one. She showed up the next day with a gift wrapped in biodegradable rice paper, looking sporty and healthy. She was carrying Lucas in a state-of-the-art sports trekker from Mountain Co-op, having taken him hiking alongside the icy Don River. Now fast asleep, Lucas's head drooped out of the trekker like a sunflower too heavy for its stalk.

Ellie separated herself from the trekker and lowered Lucas onto the bed via a fascinating series of *Don't wake up the baby* contortions, and then slouched into the armless silk chair recently inhabited by Mae.

"I'm so exhausted. I just want to divorce Gavin right now and marry my doula."

"Oh, don't do that," I muttered, rubbing my forehead.

"He's such a dink. He's never changed a single diaper,

he won't make me dinner, he almost wouldn't take Lucas to the Raffi concert today."

"To the what?"

Ignoring my question, she switched into her Dumb Guy voice, circa Manhattan 1995: "Uhuhuh, I am wiped from covering the Raptors all week, I need to *wind down* when I get home. Why should I parent when I have to run around every day while you lie on your ass in bed with your boobs hanging out."

"Maybe he's jealous of the baby nursing?" I offered, tentatively sounding out Mae's theory of the universe.

"Oh I wish," Ellie said, fiddling with her braid. "He's never even noticed my breasts. He's an ass man. I can breast-feed until I'm blue in the face as far as he's concerned. He just doesn't want to have to do any housework."

"Would you breast-feed for five years?"

"What for?"

"I don't know, I suppose to give your child optimal nutrition, and a pathological sense of being smothered?"

"I'd go for two years again, if I have another one. That gives them more than enough access to antibodies and nutrients. I just find it easy, it's sterile, it's portable, it's cheap, and if I want to go out or drink wine I can always pump."

I studied her pensively. Why was this so easy for Ellie? What was her secret? Had she made some sort of deal with the Mother Goddess where she got to have no more collateral damage from motherhood than an altered fashion sense, at the fairly reasonable cost of marrying Gavin?

"So," she urged, smiling, "open your present."

"Right." I rummaged through the rice paper and pulled out an intriguing assembly of plastic tubes and cups. It looked like a chemistry set.

"What's this?" I asked, bemused.

"A Medela double-barreled electric breast pump," she exclaimed. "You can go it at with both breasts at the same time! And then you and Calvin get to go to Las Vegas for the weekend."

"Oh. Okay, great." Visions of having to drain myself with machinery before hopping on the red-eye to Vegas blundered about confusingly in my head. "Couldn't I just give him formula?"

"Well, it's obviously your choice," she said lightly. "But to me, there's a reason Natalie Angiers called breast milk 'holy' in *The New York Times*."

I thought about this. It struck me that Ellie's peculiar maternal neurosis had to do with food. Food and toxins and germs and antibodies and pollution. Bodily pollution. I wondered what it meant for her, this fear.

"What on earth are you doing?" my mother asked in alarm when she encountered me that evening, bent over Penny's coffee table in the living room attempting to extract my breasts from the immovable suction cups of the breast pumps by dabbing at them with butter.

"What does it look like I'm doing?" I asked sourly. "I tried using the pump and it vibrated me like a bloody dentist's drill for an hour and now I can't get it off."

"Why don't you just feed the baby directly?"

"I want to go to Las Vegas."

"Well, you can give him formula, for heaven's sake."

"No I can't, he'll lose IQ points."

"Oh, that's just nonsense." She took off her coat, folded it crisply, and disappeared into the kitchen, reemerging with a butter knife, which she slipped into the breast pump cup to break the suction.

"This is just a disturbing version of *Last Tango in Paris*," I said.

"Well then, don't immerse yourself in so much paraphernalia," she retorted. "Thank goodness I didn't have to struggle with all this guilt when I bottle-fed you and your brother. It doesn't seem to have done you any harm."

Of course, it wasn't just the breast-feeding that was hideously fraught, it was the role. The role of motherhood. There appeared to be a variety of models to choose from. I hadn't considered that before. The prospect had seemed stark before, but clear. How to be a mother: Have a baby. Figure out where to put the crib, and resume editing manuscripts by Michael Ignatieff as soon as the baby is old enough to go away. That's more or less what my mother did, as far as I can tell, and it "didn't appear to do me any harm." Now along came Mae and Ellie, who took quite the opposite tack, wanting all the Michael Ignatieffs and manuscripts to go away.

Motherhood also made the good-looking refrigerator repairman go away, at least as I think back on it now. The fridge man came by one morning to find out why Freon was leaking into the vegetable crisper. He was very handsome, this fridge man, with lively green eyes and fine bones and a rear end like Bruce Springsteen's. Having ushered him in, I followed him around the house inquiring politely about appliances, offered him coffee, leaned gracefully against the wall with my hip jutting out the way I always had, all my grown-up life, in the company of good-looking men. A girl at ease with herself, my body language said. And he, this fridge man, didn't demur at all. Indeed, he was the soul of discretion, for somehow he had collected himself sufficiently, in the instant that I opened the door, to neither stare at nor point out to me that my shirt was undone and the left flap of my nursing bra was dangling down, exposing the sullen, heavy bomb that was a lactating breast with a nipple strung too low.

"Thanks for your help," I sing-songed as he made his way down our front walk. At which point I happened to glance down at myself, and staggered backward like an electrocuted cat.

The Thing About Motherhood

"Look, the thing about motherhood," said Maureen, who I hadn't seen since our last prenatal class, "is that you cannot surrender to the weird, sentimental ideology that surrounds it. Don't wallow in it, Frannie. Don't let it make you forget to button up your shirt."

Maureen had had a scheduled cesarean at the end of November, popped out twin girls, handed them and a crate of Similac to her plucky husband Albert, and dashed back to work at the Ministry of Finance.

"Motherhood is just a part of your life. It's just one of your jobs." She was wandering about the living room examining the décor, fascinated by Penny's taste.

"What's that sticking out of the back of your jacket?" I asked.

"What?" She peered over her shoulder, inspecting her black cashmere Ports blazer.

"It looks . . . I think it's a coat hanger."

"Oh hell," said Maureen. She burst out laughing and sat down, tapping her cell phone against her forehead. "I just sat through a cabinet priorities meeting and nobody said a goddamn word."

She tried to stuff the hanger into her Cole-Haan purse, to no avail, and then slid it indecisively onto the couch beside her. "That's so patronizing of them not to comment, I can't believe it. Don't tell dumbo mum she's got furniture in her clothes." She straightened up, and threw back her shoulders. "They don't get it. I'm fighting for a cause."

"Which is what?"

"Which is to stay on track, stay beautiful, stay intellectually stimulated, and let Albert be the daddy. Why not?"

"I don't know. I guess . . . *hear hear*," I offered.

She shrugged and patted her hair. "So I have more on my plate. I forget a few appointments. I still weigh a thousand pounds." She sprang back up and strode to the mirror in the hallway, scrutinizing herself crossly. "Actually, I'm a whale."

"You are not a whale."

Maureen was not a whale. She was maybe a size eight like me, only taller. She could get away with bell-bottoms, which she wore paired with a fashionable '70s blouse and square-toed shoes, plus one or two unintended accessories like a Pinocchio sticker. Once, she came to prenatal class with a partially eaten lollypop dangling from her bottom. Her husband's purpose, apparently, was to discreetly point these things out and applaud as she struggled valiantly to retain focus while parenting three children under five.

"Anyway, I brought you something." She retrieved a shopping bag from the hallway and pulled out a box. "It's an educational mobile. It'll sharpen Lester's faculties while he's lying around on his back."

That afternoon, Calvin put the mobile together and hung it from the bedroom ceiling so that it dangled over the baby's basket. It was black and white—very important for babies, for some reason—and consisted of big, bold patterns. One of the circular disks on the mobile depicted a simple, staring face. Lester studied it with avid interest, as if reading the newspaper.

"Maureen says this mobile is very popular," I offered.

"Is that so?" answered Calvin, twirling it contemplatively. "I guess those images imprint pretty deeply in babies' psyches." He thought about this.

"Twenty-five years from now, I'm going to stick that face on a campaign poster and run for Parliament, and everyone born in the nineties is going to vote for me, and they won't know why."

I hugged him, grateful for a quip, which returned him to someone I knew. He looked at me, smiling. "How's that for a career plan?"

"It's brilliant. What are you going to do in the meantime?"

"I have absolutely no idea."

Lamentations

"Help!"

"This is 911, how may I direct your call?"

"My baby has been shrieking for three weeks!"

"Calm down, ma'am, are you in your nightie?"

"I've been in my nightie for a month! I can't remember what pants feel like."

"Is there another adult with you?"

"Yes, but he has ceased to function and merely weeps."

"Ma'am, have you consulted Dr. Spock?"

"Dr. Spock can sod off, that glib old fart, he hasn't got a clue!"

"Have you gone off gassy foods like broccoli?"

"I'm eating nothing but soybeans and grass."

"All right, ma'am, I suggest that you stay on your diet. Now take the baby to a dark, soundproofed room and rock him gently until your hips pop out of their sockets."

"Okay . . ."

New parents are tender, smitten fools who think they've got this baby thing under control at the two-week mark. They stop putting the diapers on backwards and get used to sleep deprivation; they sort out breast-feeding and begin to venture out to cafés. They phone their friends: "This isn't so bad. Johnny's, like, a totally easy baby. We're just doing what we always do." La la la . . .

Ka boom.

Johnny bursts forth with a spectacular bout of bawling that lasts, unabated, for three months.

Darkness descends.

All that winter, in the dreadful, drawn-out hours of night this baby, our son, shrilled like a smoke alarm from midnight until the reluctant dawn. We moved without intermission from one scenario of outrage to another: the cruel torture of the diaper change, the unspeakable hor-ror of a bath, the unutterable torment of feeling peckish, the terrifying specter of mummy's face. The lamentations crowded everything out: sleep, desire, kindness.

Sometimes, when I held Lester aloft, he jammed his lit-tle fists together and flung back his head, resembling, for all the world, a tiny Italian opera singer mourning the death of Aida. I would study him frantically, maddened by my helplessness: "What is the bloody matter? What?" Calvin and I became miserable partners in the all-engrossing mission of making the baby content. We

plopped him in a mechanical swing, we swayed him in a
Snugli, we hoarsely croaked songs which were drowned
out by his cries, so that we wound up, in essence, shout-
ing them at him: *Hush little baby don't you cry. Mama da da
da da apple pie.*

We stuck his basket in the bathroom and boldly let him
wail for ten minutes, absolutely sick with guilt, until we
couldn't stand it anymore and rushed to the rescue. We
lost it. I'd storm off to the patio and stand there in the
freezing dark with a Wagnerian soundtrack of *stürm und
drang* thundering in my head, then shuffle back in to
dully stuff my face with McCain's Deep 'N' Delicious
Vanilla Cake in a fit of pure self-loathing.

Calvin escaped via Kevin, who had to chase squirrels
daily in Riverdale Park, enabling his temporary master to
smoke hash spliffs behind elm trees and tap melancholi-
cally on his djembe.

We discovered that my brother's bed had a gadget that
could be switched on to make the entire heart-shaped
mattress vibrate, like the ones built to promote sad sexual hijinks in motels. Calvin would drape Lester across
his chest and lie down and be vibrated for two hours at a
stretch with an expression of profound stoicism on his
unshaven face, light bouncing off his spectacles as they
shook.

Alternatively, at Ellie's suggestion, we ran the vacuum
cleaner to soothe Lester with white noise, wandering
about the house, drunk with sleeplessness, vacuuming
up lint and dust and air and random objects, like one of
Penny's crystal figurines and a gas bill. Eventually, since

183

we had to keep vacuuming for the duration of Lester's nap, the target became all the little brown moths that had infested the kitchen courtesy of the large sacks of flour I'd bought for the millennium. I could spend a solid hour sucking them out of the air midflight, one by one. ("What on earth are you doing?" my mother asked one day, when she arrived with some books about infant brain development and interrupted me stalking the moths, hose ablazing.

"I don't really know," I hollered above the noise. My mother bent down and switched off the Hoover. "It's the sound that soothes babies, Frances, not the *act* of vacuuming. You don't actually have to vacuum up airborne insects."

We were residents of a spick-and-span lunatic asylum, Calvin and I. There was no coherent conversation, no intimate probing, no planning our lives. Our verbal exchanges were nothing but a scattershot series of tersely spat sentences.

"Just *hold* the baby for a *minute* while I go to the bathroom."

"I *need* a glass of *ginger ale.*"

"Maybe he's *hungry.*"

"I *think* he's had enough *rocking.*"

"You're *go*-ing to *drop* him."

"You are an asshole," I said one night, waking Calvin up merely to impart that particular message. What did I mean? I don't even know. I think I wanted to say it to Lester.

"Don't you *ever* say that to me again," Calvin threatened the next morning, glaring at me with dark, hollow eyes. His expression was so taut with fury that it frightened me. I slapped him. He wobbled and then rubbed his cheek methodically. "I knew you were going to do that," he said.

"I'm sorry."

"You should be."

Everything shocked us.

After a time, Calvin developed a kind of agoraphobia that sprang from no longer knowing how to be in the world. He was too unnerved to venture out of doors with Lester, who would invariably begin screaming. For Calvin, who was accustomed to presenting himself as quietly detached and laconic, this feral infant behavior triggered an identity crisis. Thus it was that a trip to the supermarket one afternoon in February brought him to the brink of panic, and he bolted.

He had emerged from the house into the sharp winter sunlight with huge trepidation, peering out from beneath his fedora and clutching Lester gingerly, as if the baby were an unpredictable whoopee cushion. "I'm going to Loblaw's, and I'm in a hurry," Calvin barked at the aged and bespectacled cabdriver when the fellow pulled up, and stared dubiously at his prospective passengers. Once father and son were ensconced, the driver obligingly sped off, wheels spraying snow as he turned his spring-loaded Chevy down Parliament Street. Two men and a hot potato.

Once at Loblaw's, Calvin placed the sleeping baby in the complimentary baby seat in his cart, and then whizzed up and down the aisles in a race against the clock, accumulating a stalk of fennel here, a hunk of Stilton there, some fish sticks, two blueberry pies. His anxiety was a rich tapestry of existential threads: what am I, Calvin Puddie, experimental percussionist, doing in Loblaw's? How am I supposed to choose between sixteen indistinguishable brands of frozen peas? And when will my cart begin wailing?

He'd made it into a slow-moving line for the checkout counter without incident when Lester stirred, prompting Calvin to stiffen and hold his breath, glancing nervously around him; Lester opened his eyes, felt a little warm in his snowsuit, and began howling as if someone had dipped him in molten lead. Terrified yet resolute, Calvin tried to ignore him, determined to get the Stilton, lentils, and orange juice onto the counter and paid for before attending to his son.

His stance, taken together with his unshaven chin, rough Doc Martens, and off-kilter fedora, elicited all sorts of repressed-yet-pointed stares from the concerned citizenry of Toronto, wondering if they shouldn't call the child abuse hotline. A curly-headed senior standing hunched behind Calvin in the line put her Metamucil down on the counter and reached for Lester. "May I?" she asked, staring at Calvin hard, on the verge of high indignation, in case he was planning to whack the baby on the head with a stalk of fennel.

"I am fine, and he is fine," Calvin growled. He yanked his son out of his seat and held him in one arm, where Lester went purple with rage, while throwing the remaining groceries on the counter. The line of his jaw clenched and unclenched. He stormed home and burst through the door.

"I can't do this anymore." He unpacked the baby and handed him to me with an air of finality. I took Lester to the couch, latched him onto The Breast and ran my free hand through disheveled hair.

"What are you talking about?"

"I'm not doing this anymore. I'm going out."

Those were his choices? Being a father, or going out? I suppose that's exactly what his choices were.

"I want to go to New York for the weekend," he said, as portentously as if he were announcing that he planned to kill us all. "Gim is playing at Fez."

"Fine," I retorted, feeling hotly betrayed. "Get out."

"Don't tell me to get out."

"Okay, unpack the groceries and then get out."

He stomped around the house, assigning groceries to cupboards and stuffing his rucksack full of T-shirts. Then he shot me a look that was guilt-ridden yet defiant, and got out.

"Don't go," I cried out belatedly, as his Harley trundled westward past the Victorian rowhouses on Carleton Street. I stood for a long time on my brother's steps with my arms crossed tightly and a keen wind icing through my koala bear bathrobe, as bereft and undefended as any woman on any stoop in the world, watching her man go to war, or to work, or to Fez in New York to see Gim play.

A Woman's Work

"All right," I said to myself. "So what? I'm a woman. Women do this. Women do this so often that nobody even remarks upon it. It is never the plot of a novel, that a woman is left alone in the house for the weekend with her baby. Nobody considers it dramatic enough even to mention, and therefore, it is not dramatic. It is unremarkable. I am going to go inside now, and have an unremarkable time."

A brief list of unremarkable things to do in the company of a colicky infant:

Run a bath. Accomplish the amazing feat of getting one leg wet before the baby starts bawling. Retreat.

Attempt to slice potatoes one-handed whilst holding the sobbing infant at your chest with the other hand. Fail.

Exercise the dog by way of standing in the back doorway and zinging a strip of beef jerky into the far end of the yard so that his appetite obliges him to trot.

Place your baby in his basket, and watch him for seven hours straight, in the event that he inexplicably perishes if you let down your guard.

Having done so, proceed to accidentally lock him in your parents' borrowed Buick Regal with the keys in the ignition. Panic. Attempt to jimmy the door open with readily available items, such as a pussywillow stem. Release a stream of unhinged curses that would be worthy of Captain Haddock. Call 911. Have baby rescued from your gross ineptitude by a full complement of firemen, police officers, and paramedics.

Discover Mae Givens knocking on the door, and hide behind the couch on your hands and knees, refusing to be exposed to a model of cheerful and competent motherhood.

Discover that your own mother has gone off to a conference in San Francisco on feminist perspectives on psychotherapy and is not available to bail you out.

Call Ellie, and as casually as you can, try to suss out the conventional wisdom about when, exactly, it becomes necessary to take a baby to emergency after you incorrectly strap on a Snugli and he plummets to the floor.

After a few episodes of dry mouth and heart palpitations, begin tentatively to relax, provided that you and Lester repair to the bedroom and remain there at all times subsisting on nothing but Stilton.

190

Lie in bed propped up by two pillows and all of your sister-in-
  law's silk dupioni sofa cushions, cradle the suckling baby,
  whose head keeps slipping into the crevices between pillows,
  and talk to Marina on the phone.

"If you run into Calvin this week, shoot him in the
head."

"Why?"

"He's a deserter."

"Romance not going so well, huh?"

"Romance has nothing to do with it."

"Why not?"

"Because this isn't about romance. This isn't about
dining on oysters and making love. This is about being so
tense and overwhelmed that at any moment you could
fly apart like a thwacked piñata."

"Oh," says Marina.

Notice, at this point, that the baby's head has become
wedged between the underside of your mattress-sized
breast and the wall. "Gotta go."

Talk a lot about the weather. Since these conversations take
  place with Lester, they go something like this:

"Hiiiiiiiiii pooh-pooh, hellooooo, helloooo, is that a smile? Yes
  it is! *Hiiiiiiii. We're going to go outside, yes we are, because
  it's going to be* fifteen *today, isn't it? Hiiiiiiiiii . . ."*

Learn precisely what temperature it is at all times by flipping
  back and forth between CNN and the Weather Channel
  while you breast-feed. Has the forecast changed since the last

time you looked? Maybe it has, maybe it's actually going to be one degree cooler or warmer than they thought. They could have been wrong, ten minutes ago, when they forecast a high of nine degrees with rain.

Ask yourself what you are looking for. What information are you seeking? Something certain, a shift that's decisive, a spike in the temperature, a change from red light to green. A permission that you can't find within yourself, to go forth in the world, to proceed.

Penny's Library

One afternoon as the rain slanted down into the dead, brown garden, I found myself contemplating a locked door in the basement of my brother's house. It led, I knew from David, to Penny's "private library," which I was strictly forbidden to disturb. Naturally, this made me wonder what she kept in there: not books, surely. Maybe magic spells. Or a severed head. I couldn't imagine Penny getting up to anything remotely nefarious. Still, you never knew about people. I looked at the silent white door, concealing its Bluebeard secrets. Maybe David hadn't taken Penny with him to London at all, but had imprisoned her here in this room, or walled her up, like an Edgar Allan Poe villain.

Finding the scenario irresistible, I ran back upstairs and rummaged around in the kitchen drawers for a promising-looking key. After some effort, and several nervous checks on my sleeping son, I found the right key in Penny's bureau drawer and returned to the basement to reward my curiosity.

I was rewarded with a vista of Barbies.

"Oh for God's sake," I murmured. The little room was wallpapered in scarlet and had, in lieu of bookshelves to surround the antique escritoire at its center, a series of glass display cases. The room's Barbie population was arranged on all of these shelves in fastidious little tableaux. Barbie and Francie at the beach. Skipper on horseback. Barbie on a scooter. Francie in a ball gown. Barbie getting married to Ken—that wondrous tabula rasa of the male psyche who doesn't possess any genitals.

Upon the escritoire, Penny had placed the ten or twelve books that she owned. I doubted her library would give me any insight into my predicament, but I shut the library door, as if I might get caught, and sat down to play with her Barbie 'n' Book collection. They got me thinking about Penny, and Penny's brain, and what I myself might learn from thinking like Penny.

For instance, what would I learn if I cracked open *365 Ways to Change Your Life*, by überBarbie Suzanne Somers? She has children and breast cancer and relationship challenges, no? And here she has written a book, so she must have something to say.

I flipped to page one. "Today," Somers started grandly, "begin this journey to look within, searching for the answer to the two great questions: who am I, and what do I want?"

Generally speaking, I tend to associate this pair of questions with the look on Kevin's face when he's standing at the top of the staircase, gazing aimlessly into space, suffering from what appears to be a complete collapse of purpose. Nevertheless, I pondered these questions as I nipped upstairs and made some tea. Who am I? The answer turned out to be surprisingly complicated and horrifying, so I moved along. What do I want? Pretty much everything, really, except for infant colic and a poke in the eye with a hot stick.

I took the tea back downstairs. Somers, I discovered, had a thought for every day of the year. Here's what to think on Day 66: "The next time I read comments from some beautiful model saying she drinks enormous amounts of water daily, I will smile to myself, knowing that at that moment God is talking to me, using her as an instrument of instruction." Wha'?

I leafed ahead. Anything about motherhood? Here's the Thought for Day 81: "I can't fight aging. It is something that happens to everyone. There is no facelift, no liposuction, no breast implants, that will save me from the fate of all living things."

By the time I reached thought number 365, I realized that I'd thought all the things that preoccupy Southern California sitcom actresses. Arguably, therefore, I had become a Southern California sitcom actress. Ergo, my life had changed. That wasn't so hard.

What else did Penny read? I knew that she had been casting about for things to do after failing to finish her MBA. Although my mother had suggested volunteering at a rape crisis center or working at a soup kitchen, she apparently got caught up in other pursuits, such as . . . this was interesting: *How to Have an Out-of-Body Experience in 30 Days.*

I wouldn't have thought that thirty days was enough time to disembody myself and go floating around the universe, but according to the book it's all a matter of focus. The key to a quick departure from one's corpse, other than being shot, is to spend at least two hours each day following the book's preparatory exercises. During the first week, as near as I could make out, students spend an inordinate amount of time contemplating the feel of their tongues in their mouths. One day, for example, they're supposed to stare at themselves naked in the mirror and think about how the inside of their cheeks taste.

Another day, they are encouraged to spend an afternoon at the elephant house of their local zoo, pondering smells. "Unbutton your top button or pull out your collar and put your nose inside of it so that you can smell your skin. Does the inside of your shirt smell different than the outside?"

"Why, yes, so it does!" I imagined Penny proclaiming. "I can't wait to tell my husband!"

"Hi, honey, how was your day?"

"Well, it was extraordinary, actually. I discovered that I smell quite different than an elephant! And furthermore, I'm about to leave my body and become 'a pure and formless point of awareness in space'!"

"Honey, you know, I've been thinking about how you

don't have a lot to do, now that you've dropped out of business school . . ."

"If you're like many OBEers," the authors announced, "you may eventually feel as though you have more control over the course of your OBEs than you do over many of the events in your everyday life."

Oh, I could see trouble brewing there. "Screw this for a lark," Penny probably thought, in the midst of a passionate dispute with David about the upholstery. "I'm outta here to float on the ceiling." Some people call this escapism, commonly associated with other isms—like alcoholism, workaholism, and going-out-to-gamble-at-the-casinoism. I recall it, in my teenage years, as a fondness for doing hits of Purple Microdot.

Funny. All these months I'd been plotting to fetch my life back as frantically as a dog scrabbling up a cliff face, and now, for the first time, I wondered what my life would have become without Lester—merely an idle reflection upon itself, doomed to remain at its smooth, gleaming surface.

Or was that just Penny?

Just then I thought I heard Lester crying. I jumped up and scurried to the door, only to find that it was locked or jammed from the outside. I rattled the handle furiously and pounded on the wood with my fists. "I'm coming, Lester," I cried. I kicked at the door, and twisted the knob again, trying to quell my panic. "Don't worry, sweetie!" You'd think a dingo was making off with the baby. And then, irate as a mother bear, I began to pelt the door with Barbies. *Thud* went a vintage Barbie in an orange pantsuit, *whack* went a bikini-clad Francie. All at once, the door flew open. There was Calvin, with our son nestled calmly in his arms. A Ken doll glanced off his cheekbone and flew headlong into an old umbrella stand.

"What the hell are you doing?"

"Oh my God, I'm so glad to see you. You have no idea!" I threw my arms around his neck. "I was just trapped in Penny's brain."

He kissed me passionately, Lester cradled carefully to one side, even as he chuckled. "Well then, consider yourself rescued, my love."

When Nothing Is Wrong

Calvin had returned from his richly lived days in New York filled with an enthusiasm and levity that swiftly dissipated in the oppressive uncertainty of our lives until, as March melted into April, he slipped almost imperceptibly into depression.

In truth, this was hard to spot, because he's a man, and men don't tend to mention that they're depressed. They just, very gradually, dematerialize and recede into their chairs. It's a confusing process. If they aren't talkative to begin with, whereas you blather nonstop, it takes a while to notice that they're not listening to you with engagement but are, in fact, simply staring at formless points of light in space. Then, of course, when the revelation finally hits you, and you confront them, they deny it, which for women, means having to play interminable and ultimately futile games of Twenty Questions.

"What's wrong, honey?"

"Nothing."

"Really? Well, I can't pin it down, but I feel like something's bothering you, because you haven't eaten, spoken, left the house or even risen from that chair in two weeks, and I'm just wondering if anything's wrong."

"No."

"Are you depressed?"

"No."

"You're not troubled that professional baseball players make so much more money than you do, are you?"

"No."

"Are you sad because I'm fat?"

"No."

By the twentieth stab-in-the-dark question, the man relents somewhat, expanding his response from "no" to "I'll be fine." This effectively ends the conversation, as the mother/wife/daughter trails off by saying: "Well . . . let me know if you want to talk about it . . ."

I think this is why women become excessively analytical about the opposite sex. It's not that they're more interested in gossip and romance. It is that they have no choice but to wild-guess their way around the stolid silences of males. Little girls watch their mothers trying to eke monosyllables out of their fathers, and learn the finer strategic techniques of moving males beyond "I'll be fine," with the rare, brilliant tactician actually scoring a full confession, such as "I have an earache," or "I got fired."

I was aiming, of course, for a confession about his

schemes for escape. Possibly even a revelation about another woman. Something was up, I figured, because there was about as much spark between us as you might get with two wet socks. But all I got was occasional muttering, under duress, about dashed hopes for ever playing again with the Garden Snakes, and how teaching percussion to Serb immigrants and north Toronto high school students was tantamount to drowning slowly in a vat of molasses.

"You've had an affair, haven't you?" I persisted a few nights later. I had to shout, because we were on a date at Dora Keogh pub on the Danforth—courtesy of my mother. The place was jammed with sweating revelers celebrating the end of the workweek.

"I am not going to dignify that with a response," Calvin shouted back. He studied me skeptically, leaning forward to sip the froth from his beer. I took his calm defiance as an invitation to speculate freely.

"Is it that French woman? The one you met on your tour, who couldn't stand to be away from you long enough for you to, at least, see your son through his first year?"

He continued staring at me.

"Or it's what's-her-face, isn't it," I charged on. "That accordion player for the Garden Snakes who couldn't carry a tune. You fell in love with her out of pity."

"You're just holding it against me that I had a good time in New York," he argued. "You stayed here and had a shitty time, while I got to go away and have fun. That's all that this is about."

"No it's not. It's about the fact that *you* are a suspected philanderer."

I noticed that the bartender had grown interested in our conversation and kept shooting us glances to keep himself posted while otherwise sloshing pints of ale to eager, outstretched hands.

"This is by far the stupidest conversation I've ever had," Calvin said, shoving back his bar stool. He pushed through the crowd of swaying, singing Irishmen to find the men's bathroom. I remained at the bar, nursing my tepid pub wine—heady stuff, though, after months and months. I fell almost jubilantly into the thrall of my suspicions.

The Other Woman was tall. For sure. She was tall, and she had tiny little flat perky prepubescent breasts. She was plain, too, wasn't she? She would have to be, because men never betray you for an irresistible beauty, that's too explicable. It's the first thing you seize upon, that he's run off with some psychopathic snake with big hair, and it's always wrong. The Other Woman startles with her neither-here-nor-there-ness, her pallid personality and unremarkable allure. She's the worst sort of insult that way, slapping you in the face with her plainness. She probably even has children. How galling.

"Is it Theresa?" I demanded, when he returned and hopped back onto his stool. "That loopy space cadet of a waitress? I should have known the first time I went to El Teddy's with you and you ogled her ass."

"You're being psychotic," he observed.

I slumped forward, leaning my elbows on the bar. Perhaps this was, in fact, completely deranged. But I was fishing for something true; it was just hard to know what, and impossible to articulate. I was living in an experience for which I had no vocabulary, this displacement of romance in the turmoil of childbirth. Where did I go, I was wanting to ask him, and what claim do I have on you, what's my potency, now that my face resembles a boiled ham? Maybe I was haunted by the ghosts of former lovers, who took off under far less provocative circumstances than these. Touch without faith. Suppress all expressions of hope as bad manners.

"There's no reason for me to trust you," I ventured. "I don't really know you."

"What if there's nothing to know?" he challenged, pushing his fedora back from his sweating forehead. "What if I'm like the gardener in that movie *Being There?*" he drummed percussively on his knee and scanned the room. He wouldn't look at me. "There's no secret chamber in my head that you're going to unlock, Frannie. All there is in there"—he tapped on his temple— "is hockey scores and jazz riffs."

I regarded him dubiously. "Then why have you been depressed, if you're such a simpleton?"

He shrugged, and took a sip of his beer. "Because what makes me happy is music. Playing music, you know? It's not hugely ambitious. I was happy in New York with the Snakes. I don't know how to be happy living in someone else's house with, like, zebraskin rugs and creepy Barbie doll collections. And those crystal unicorns that are just so . . . uhuhuh"—he shivered—"what are those about? And I love Lester, I do, but he keeps covering me in vomit and splitting my eardrums. It's like, babies are very hostile. I'm not used to loving someone who I fantasize about zinging into space with a catapult."

I started to laugh. He gestured futilely. "He's a baby. We don't have anything in common."

"You have me in common," I said. Good news, or bad?

He settled his gaze on me. "Yeah. That's true. We do. You're the prize. You came in an exploding package, but you're still the prize."

"Why?" I didn't understand it, I really didn't.

"Because this is it, Frannie, this is the deal." He kissed me, and I pondered him, uncertain still, not wholly appeased, perhaps even a little astonished.

I Don't Know How She Does It

"Perhaps your anxieties would diminish if either you or Calvin got a job," my mother said, idly thumbing her way through the latest edition of the *Guardian*. She was sitting in her living room with her feet crossed at the ankles, licking her thumb before turning each page, which for some reason I found highly irritating. I suppose I was on edge. As per the subject she'd raised: Terrifying Conversation Alert.

"We don't *not* have jobs," I argued. "Calvin is teaching music, and I'm doing those bits for *Toronto Life*. Plus, I'm on board to edit another *Pithy Review* article." Indeed, I was dragging the prospect around like a security blanket. I am still here, I did not die.

"You can't afford rent," she retorted, without looking up.

"Well, what sort of a job am I supposed to get in

Toronto?" Help, help, the tundra. "And what am I supposed to do with Lester?" He was sleeping in my lap. I
loved him like this, all warm and quiet, the little pie. His
colic had vanished overnight, as if it had just been a practical joke. Now Calvin wore him all over town and had
turned himself into a chick magnet.

My mother peered at me over her reading glasses.
"You could apply to one of the newspapers. There are
four of them in the city, after all. In a raging war, I hear.
Hiring like mad. They doubtless have on-site day care."

"Oh, aaargh!" I replied, eloquently. My mother was so
brutally practical. She had no sense of how difficult it
was for me to reconcile the disparate threads of my life,
the ambitions, the dreams, the little son, the scarily im-
pecunious man.

"Look, Frances," she ventured, "we can never acquire
enough perfect resolve before we decide to act, because
life itself intervenes. Life is impatient." She folded up the
Guardian and put it on the coffee table. "The immigrants
I counsel have learned that. They're under no apprehension that they have control over their fate."

"I didn't know you counseled immigrants."

"Well, I run a support group for a few depressed
Bosnians." She smoothed her skirt. "A Rwandan fellow
joined us recently, and a woman from Beijing. I was an
immigrant myself, of course, so I sympathize. They're
just as anxious as you are, Frances, about their displacement. One of my patients was a Pakistani fellow who felt
overwhelmed by Torontonians' sense of privacy. I mean,
there are thirty million of us in an enormous country. You

don't think about it. He was so homesick he kept rushing down to the Eaton Centre just to stand in a crowd."

"That's interesting," I said. "On the other hand, I'm not an immigrant."

"Perhaps not, but you're behaving like one."

I sighed and ruffled Lester's downy hair. "What do you suggest that I do?"

"Well now, Freddie," my father interjected, having puttered into the living room and overheard the tail end of the conversation. "Why don't you talk to Mary Scoretti? I don't know if you met her, but she's married to my colleague Jack, the fellow who wanted you to edit his book proposal about Ontario fishing clubs. You remember. His wife is a sort of personal consultant."

"Oh, please."

He looked hurt. "There's no need to roll your eyes. Here you are in Toronto raising a family. You could talk to someone about what the landscape here is for you, or perhaps how you might get back to New York." He clasped his hands behind his back and rocked on his heels, casting apprehensive glances at my mother in a quest for support.

The next week, at his behest, my mother left a clipping from the classified section of the *Toronto Globe & Mail* on my pillow, advertising the services of Mary Scoretti, "Life Consultant."

A Fruitful Conversation

Mary and Jack Scoretti lived in a high-rise condo on Avenue Road with a hyper little West Highland terrier, who was out at the groomer's the first time I came. We broke the ice at the door by talking about her dog, with whom she was clearly smitten. I assumed she would notice the random tufts of dog fur festooning my blazer and zero in on that as an indication that I was too unkempt for the work force. But instead of sizing me up, she seemed timid and flustered, and hastened to offer me coffee. I sat down in her white, plush-carpeted living room and waited, having not the slightest idea what to expect from a life consultant.

"Here we are," she said, scurrying back in, handing me a mug, and settling her plump bottom into a chair. She had looked more businesslike in her brochure photo, in expensive clothes and a short, severe haircut. In person, she was almost disheveled: dressed in roomy cotton drawstring pants and sandals, her face friendly and owlish and faintly forlorn.

We talked back and forth in a curiously aimless fashion, until she apparently felt comfortable enough to reveal that she was struggling with lung disease. Then, leaving that hanging there like a clanging church bell, she said: "So, what can I do for you?"

I choked back that feeling I get when I'm talking to therapists or counselors that *it's none of their business,* and explained that I was basically at cross purposes. I envisioned an untenable future for myself, for I longed to return to New York and yet I wasn't sure what that meant anymore, now that I was a mother. And I was hardly married to a banker, was I? That Bohemian lifestyle, those cocktail parties and mornings in cafés, the seminars at the 92nd Street Y, the films at MOMA. How could I pull it all off with a child? And yet I was driven, you see, and here I was in the provinces!

"Like, I just read the latest *New Yorker,*" I offered by way of example, "and I thought: Oh my God, I am never going to edit this magazine. I'm not even going to be an editorial intern at this magazine. Those editors are at the center of the universe leading their elegant lives, and I am on Pluto. How did they get to the center of the universe while I wound up on Pluto? There is no getting famous on Pluto. If Shakespeare had lived on Pluto he would have received nothing but rejection letters. 'Thank you for sending your play *Hamlet* by intergalactic express, but it doesn't work for us. Because you live on Pluto.' "

I prattled on like this, how there must be a way around the obstacles, a way to make sense of my situation, perhaps even find a really interesting job here in Toronto, if she knew of any. "What is ambition, anyway?" I wondered. "Who says ambition is foiled outside New York? The Beothuk Indians who lived in Newfoundland for a thousand years weren't aware of a world without snow and the sea. An ambitious Beothuk wouldn't feel compelled to move to New York, would he? His ambition would be to fuse spiritually with a bear or something. There's no objective standard for what fulfills ambition. You know?"

She nodded. "I see the problem, yes." She assigned me some homework. I was, first of all, to choose what shape I liked best: square, circle, triangle, cross, or spiral. Also, for five minutes, three times a day, I was to complete the sentence: "Now I am aware of . . ." whatever. Get into the present, she explained. Hear the birds chirp, the rain fall. Focus on the present for five minutes, three times a day.

Mary went off to fetch her dog, and I went home to try my exercises. I had no preference for the shapes, so ordered them randomly and consulted the interpretation chart that Mary had provided. "The triangle is associated with pyramids, arrowheads, and sacred mountains. It carries the theme of self-discovery and revelation of goals, visions, and dreams." I made a note to myself to call Penny through the brick wall in that basement and tell her I'd discovered her ideal career.

The following week, Mary tried to get me to be aware of the present right in front of her. "What do you hear now?" she asked expectantly. I tilted my head in concentration. Just then her Westie began retching on the carpet. "Oh fuck!" she yelped. Then: "Oh, excuse me, that wasn't very professional."

I told her, diplomatically, that I was simply aware of the sound of coffee percolating in her kitchen.

"You're making an intellectual judgment," she countered, after a strategic strike on the carpet with Mr. Clean. "You're saying 'coffee' because you deduce that. But what does it sound like?"

I struggled. "Bubbling," I suggested. In my notebook, I wrote: *coffee as intellectually conceptualized vs. bubbling.*

Next she had me eat a banana. "See if you can eat a banana so that you can feel the seeds. If you eat it in total awareness, you'll feel them."

I tried to feel the seeds, to no avail. She ate a banana too, for moral support. We ate our bananas slowly, in tandem. When there was one chunk left of the pale, slightly unripe fruit, I handed her the peel. "I can't finish the last bite of food, for some reason. I always leave one bite left on my plate. My aunt does it, too. I think it has something to do with a phobia of completion." I offered this information in an effort to be helpful.

"Try saying *won't* instead of *can't*," she said. "I *won't* eat the last piece of banana."

I nodded.

"I won't have a banana," I announced to Calvin when I got home.

"No?" He looked up from Lester, who was sitting on his lap in the kitchen, mouthing a chunk of bagel. "That's cool. No problem. How about some Jack Daniels?"

The Point of the Exercise

Lester's personality continued to brighten, like light clarifying a landscape as the sun rose. My little dark-eyed son was discovering his effect upon the world, through his smile, his triumphant batting, his vibrant voice, which was every week producing a new, exclusive sound. For a time it was all drawled vowels, then solemnly and carefully uttered gurgles. He experimented with blowing raspberries, while I supplied dialogue from *Monty Python and the Holy Grail*. Calvin read him *Good Night Moon* over and over, perhaps a hundred times, before Lester ripped out the last page while practicing his grasp. "Oh no!" Calvin admonished him. "Now we won't know how it ends!"

As Lester grew he took up headquarters in an Excersaucer supplied by Annabelle, which we plopped down in the center of the living room. From here, while his father plucked out tunes on a Dobro, he behaved like a teensy Mussolini, barking commands at the dog. Sometimes, we lay face to face on the bed, and he peered up at me from beneath his chestnut hair and went "eek" and "grr" and "a-*Mon*day." He trusted me to know what he meant, so I did. I began seeing and hearing the world through him, and grew appalled by the shameless cacophony of the city, the sirens, the horns, the billboards, the disparate trails of pop music on car radios passing by. I strained to find the harmonies for him, in the twitter of birdsong or the arabesque dance of the wind in the trees.

On a fragrant morning in early May, I took him, as I often did, to Riverdale Park, where the sounds of the city were muted. He gestured upward at a dogwood tree, whose blossoms were just now unfurling. He had never seen the blooms of a tree. As best he knew, the world was landscaped like Halloween Town in *The Nightmare Before Christmas*. He had never known the delicacy of green. I lifted him up over my head, swaying slightly, so that he could grasp wonderingly at the branches.

It occurred to me that you didn't need exercises from a book to make you aware. This was awareness enough, this beauty, this reaching. You needed a child.

The Affair of the Crocque
Monsieur Sandwich Maker

One day, my ersatz mother-in-law in Cape Breton, who was equal parts hysterical with excitement over a grandchild and mortified by her son's marital status, arranged a pickup for us at The Hudson Bay department store, which Calvin went to fetch on his Harley. He came back an hour later, zooming up the driveway with a white stuffed bear the size of a wine barrel strapped to his back and listing to one side, its blue satin bow fluttering behind them.

"Oh my God," I said, when Calvin manhandled the creature into the house.

"Well, that's my mother," he said curtly.

I could not imagine Calvin's mother. He rarely spoke of her, and when he did, he was taciturn and uncomfortable, as if referring to something unpleasant from his long-ago past. I suppose I should have thought it was odd, but mired as I was in my fiascoes of displacement and parenthood, I didn't ask too many questions. His parents, or rather the absence of information about his parents, allowed for a certain distance between us to persist. I didn't want to bridge it. I wasn't married, and I saw no reason to discover what I had married into.

This policy changed one highly embarrassing evening, when David and Penny came home and declared war, forcing us to retreat from their perfect house and become wanderers on the road to Cape Breton.

In my own defense, I want to say that the Penny 'n' Davids arrived at a particularly inopportune moment, because I had run out of diapers and was just about to pin one of Penny's monogrammed Lin de Frandre hand towels on Lester when she walked out of the realm of constant jokes between me and Calvin and actually into the room.

"What are you doing in my bedroom?" she asked, in an anxious whine. She dropped her suitcase with a little thud and eyeballed the shocking developments: a baby basket, a diaper pail, a littered, crumpled bed, and Lester himself lying on a change pad on Penny's mahogany bureau, sporting . . .

Is that my towel?

"Oh . . . um . . ." I waved my free hand about vaguely.

"That's *Belgian linen*." She unzipped her jacket with a violent tug.

"I'm sorry," I said, studying the hand towel with new interest. Lester was kicking his legs in the air and swiveling his head to locate the sound of the stranger's voice.

"I ran out of diapers. I can replace it."

Penny glared at me with intense displeasure. "Could you please get that baby off my *bureau?*"

"He's not an object," I said, my embarrassment shifting to indignation. "He's your nephew." I collected Lester carefully and held him close. He peered over my shoulder, entranced by his reflection in the mirror.

"We lent you our house and you *ruined* it," Penny said, staring at me accusingly. Blood rushed to my face and I stammered, trying to come up with a suitable reply, but she didn't wait. She flew off down the hall and I could hear her opening doors and gasping. "Where's my Wax Wizard kit?" she shouted from the bathroom.

"Your what?"

"Did you wax your legs with *my* kit?"

"Oh, as if . . ." I rolled my eyes, still trembling from the unwelcome surprise of her, having expected them on the weekend. Like I have time to wax my legs. I carried Lester downstairs, wondering where, in fact, I might have put her Wax Wizard kit.

"Oh . . . right." It came to me that I might have used the Wax Wizard to fashion a kind of flypaper strip for the moths after my mother advised me against sucking them up with the vacuum cleaner hose. I sighed and kissed Lester on the head.

David was in the kitchen, fixing himself a bourbon and looking decidedly perturbed. "This is not acceptable, Frannie," he said over his shoulder when he heard me come in.

"Look, I'm sorry, I got your arrival dates mixed up."

"There's hash residue in Penny's Deluxe Croque Monsieur sandwich maker," he observed.

"Oh, is there?" I thought frantically. Had Calvin been softening his hash in an *appliance?*

"I could smell it as soon as I opened the cupboard. It's not like I wasn't a pothead in college. Is that any way to be a house guest? I hope you at least watered my grass."

"I did, yeah, I definitely did that," I offered cooperatively. Of course, it was awhile ago. Upon reflection, I hadn't seen the grass in a while. I changed the subject.

"David, come and meet your nephew."

He took a swig of his bourbon and turned to face me, cracking a grin in spite of himself as soon as he laid eyes on Lester. The baby was resting his chin on my shoulder and sucking on my hair. He gazed curiously at his uncle.

"Hey there, buddy," said David, leaning forward until the two were nose to nose. "Oh, he's pretty cute. He looks a hell of a lot like me. It's uncanny."

"You think so?" I asked, swept up in the pleasure of the introduction.

"Oh yeah, it's spooky. He's my spitting image."

"David!" Penny shrieked from upstairs. Reflexively, I began to hum an aimless little tune. Here comes some shit. In my experience, the trouble with being a mess is that you always get caught off guard, because you never know what kind of mess you've made, exactly. It seems more or less reasonable to you to use a linen hand towel as a diaper, for instance. If you'd *known,* well . . .

"There are *diapers* in my *L'esprit waste basket!"* Penny

wailed. Oh, well, so what? Calvin and I had a Diaper Genie for a while but we couldn't figure out how to use it. The waste basket was empty. Duh. It was just sitting there waiting for something to do.

Lester was reaching over my shoulder for an empty soda water bottle on the counter. I leaned in so that he could bat at it and knock it over, which struck him as a great triumph, so I set it up and he knocked it over again. This went on for some time while David consoled Penny upstairs. Calvin was out giving a drum lesson. I wished he had a cell phone.

"Where is my grass?" David came into the kitchen and stood before me with his fists clenched and his eyes flaring. "How could you do that to me, Frannie? It's not hard to water grass. It's just not hard. You killed it, and you hid it away."

"Oh, come on! That's ridiculous." How dare he make such an insulting accusation, it was so typical. "I don't know where your grass is at the moment," I said hotly. "It's just—it's been a bit hectic around here."

"Well, that's a fucking understatement. I go up to my bedroom and it looks like Toys 'R' Us. My guest room is full of crap. My wife's having a nervous breakdown. And my grass, my humble, not-very-hard-to-care-for grass has been murdered."

"No, it hasn't," I said, clinging to this one slender prospect of redemption. "Have you looked in the basement? Maybe Calvin took the bowls down to the basement and polished them or something."

He grunted and pushed open the basement door,

thudding down the steps. After a moment, he exclaimed: "What the fuck did you do that for?"

"Do what?" I shouted, hating all this staggering outrage. Trying to remember whether I had ever retrieved Ken from the umbrella stand.

He popped his head out of the basement door. "You killed my grass and replaced it with fucking *Astro*turf?"

"Okay, look," I said, tears stinging my eyes, "I did not do that. I didn't. But I'm very sorry. I'm sorry, all right? You don't know what it's like having a baby, I can no longer have a bath."

"You're using that as an excuse," my brother intoned, with his pompous sense of authority over my psyche. Granted, it was true. "It is not hard to water a couple of bowls of grass. You just don't care. You don't care about anyone but yourself."

"That's a lie. You have no idea what caring about people means, David. I'm good at that and bad at this."

He gazed at me with a characteristic mix of amusement and contempt, giving his bourbon glass a shake and cracking an ice cube with his teeth. "I'll say."

"I'm not a paragon of virtue when it comes to housesitting, Calvin, but you could have advised me that you put Astroturf in David's grass bowls."

"I'm sorry," he said, with studious indifference. "It slipped my mind."

He resumed tapping his foot in time to the rhythm of the jazz quartet we were watching at the old Rex Hotel. The lounge was crowded and dimly lit and I was pushing Lester's stroller back and forth to keep him sleeping, at risk of tripping the waiters.

"Well, *why* did you stick Astroturf in them, if you don't mind me asking?"

"Because they were stupid and pretentious and I refused to water them."

"But that's so passive aggressive. It's like the hash in the croque monsieur thing. Why didn't you just spray the house with graffiti and make your message clear?"

"I refuse to respect that kind of materialism." He also refused to look at me. I felt like pouring my beer over his head. Indeed, I had unconsciously lifted up the pint when he caught me by the wrist. "Don't take it out on me," he warned. "You're the one who made the house look like a grocery bag had exploded. The situation was untenable, and you know it."

I glared at him. "Well, so what are we going to do now?"

Obviously Penny and David were not going to rent the house to us, and that was a relief, more than anything. In our indecision, we had sunk into inertia. We had to make real plans now, had to stop playing house.

He leaned back in his chair, clasping his hands behind his head. "I do *not* know." He glanced at me sidelong. "But don't act like I'm the problem. From now on, I'm one third of the problem. You're one third, Lester's one third."

I thought about this, absently poking at the bubbles in my beer. "Maybe we should put our stuff in storage and take Lester to visit your side of his family. Maybe that will shake things up and give us a sense of direction."

He nodded. "We should."

"Maybe we could move to Cape Breton," I added, struck by this fanciful notion, "and just . . . I'm so sick of trying to solve my life. Maybe we should just move there and ditch our ambitions and live on a farm."

"You can't live on a farm," he said, returning his attention to the jazz quartet. "You'd have to do chores."

At Home in the
Clan Stanley Puddie

The more I thought about Cape Breton, as we prepared to leave my brother's perfect house and wander eastward, the more romantic the notion became for me. We could get lost, Calvin and Lester and I, in the remote and rugged beauty of the Cape Breton highlands, with its sea-misted forests and ancient hills. We could homestead on the shores of the salmon-filled Margaree River, tending to patches of root vegetables and singing mournful Gaelic songs; we could hike, we could whale-watch out on the Atlantic, Lester and I could feed peanuts to moose.

Why not? I grew enchanted by the prospect of reinventing myself this way, of casting off the shadow of my family, conquering my brother's petty materialistic fantasies and my father's armchair ambitions and my own corrosive longing for New York. I would grow braids, and find my own ease and freedom in a majestic land-scape. Calvin—why I hadn't thought of this before?—was not just a man who made not a cent and ruined sandwich makers. He was a veritable portal to a new world.

I began to read Alistair MacLeod's epic Cape Breton novel *No Great Mischief*, and daydreamed about the Clan Calum Ruadh, who set themselves upon the sea in 1792, leaving Scotland behind for a new land that would haunt and hold them through the generations. As our rental car sped through Quebec along the banks of the magnificent Saint Lawrence River, I read passages aloud. "Here's when the Clan Calum Ruadh first ar-rive," I explained to Calvin: " 'One sees the little group of people now, as if we could, in imagination's mist, rowing or sailing in their shallops across the choppy fall sea . . . When the boat landed on the graveled strand, the cousins who had written the Gaelic letter and the Mi'k-maqs who were at home in "the land of the trees" helped them ashore . . .' "

I dipped the book down. "The land of the trees," I re-peated in an appreciative murmur. *We're going to the land of the trees.*

Calvin said nothing. He'd found a radio station that played Haitian soukous music, and turned the sound down with some reluctance to let me read, leaving his hand to hover at the dial. He remained reticent about his family and the town of his birth, answering my increas-ingly excited queries with monosyllabic replies.

"Your father's father was a miner too, right?"

"Yes."

"Did they want you to go into mining?"

"No."

"Did they speak French to you when you were a kid?"

"Yes."

"Were you close to your grandparents?"

"No."

Through incessant questioning over plates of poutine in roadside diners, I managed to extract evocative glimpses of Calvin's childhood. His grandfather Audile was a towering man who smelled of coal dust and tobacco. He did vaudeville whenever the mines were closed, traveling as far down the coastline as Boston, and Calvin remembered him tap-dancing in the kitchen once, drunk on moonshine, while his other relatives clapped and laughed in the flickering light of a coal fire. His grandmother Olive prepared batches of brewis for Friday dinners, made by simmering hardtack and salt cod in a cast-iron pot.

"It was disgusting," Calvin reflected. "It tasted like oatmeal with bones."

"Did she make you eat it, though?"

"I fed it to the cat."

"What else did you eat? What are the local dishes?"

"Tuna Helper and halibut."

The Puddie clan lived on a high bluff overlooking the Atlantic, Calvin said, in a tiny clapboard house built by the mining company in a row of identical houses. All were thrown up in 1915, on six streets between cliff's edge and

Plummer Avenue, which was where the women bought supplies and gathered in the pharmacy to gossip. "My mother takes cabs from one end of Plummer Avenue to the other," Calvin added. "She says she's going 'uptown.' It's, like, two blocks."

"They still live in the same house?"

"My mother was born in the bedroom she still sleeps in."

"So you'll inherit it?"

He shrugged. "I guess so."

I contemplated that—an old clapboard house by the sea—while we drove the final miles of mainland Nova Scotia and approached the Canso causeway, the only route across to Cape Breton for modern pilgrims in rental cars. The island rose up out of the gray sea like a whale's back, as if breaking the surface to breathe before plunging back down into the bone-cold depths. It was a dark, shadowed green, covered thickly in fir trees. The only harbinger of human settlement was a Tim Hortons doughnut shop and an Irving gas station—the commercial equivalent of a Maritimes flag.

After crossing the causeway, we stopped at Tim Hortons for respite.

"Do you think Lester can digest chocolate sprinkles?"

"Why do you ask?"

"I think some just fell off my doughnut and landed in his mouth." I was holding him in my lap with his face angled up. He was watching the neon gas sign, which was slowly spinning around.

"I don't think it will kill him."

"Well, you say that, but there was a baby in England who died last month because his parents fed him salty mashed potatoes."

"How cruel." Calvin glanced at his watch. He was tired. His driving glasses were fogged up. He took them off and squeezed his eyes shut, pinching his nose.

"Look, Frannie, I'm worried that you're whipping up a fantasy about Cape Breton."

"Why do you say that?"

He sighed. "Because it's not like an Alistair MacLeod novel. It's more like a . . . like a . . ." He dropped his head into his hand and stirred his coffee desultorily, unwilling to elaborate.

"More like a what?" I prodded. "Like an Ann-Marie Macdonald novel?"

He shrugged. "Who's she?"

"You know. She wrote *Fall on Your Knees*. Epic family saga featuring incest and abuse."

Calvin drummed his fingers on the table. "It's the word *epic* getting lodged in your brain that concerns me. I think you need to let go of that idea." He leaned forward and looked me in the eyes. "My parents are not epic. Where they live is not epic. They live in a shithole. All the mines have been shut down. Everyone in the town is unemployed and drunk."

"I know it's not rich," I said, shifting Lester on my knee, as if protectively removing him from his father's revelations.

"It's not just not rich, Frannie. It's also not epic."

"Okay," I said, dubious.

Calvin sat back and gazed out the window. "Just so you know."

"Okay. I know."

Of course I didn't know. My vision of poverty was romantic. It featured hard-working men with hard stares, their hearts broken quietly by fate. It featured houses with faded exteriors, playgrounds rusted by sea breeze, white wooden churches on hilltops. It did not feature the very first thing I encountered when we drove into New Waterford, which was fire hydrants painted as Smurfs.

"Calvin!" My jaw went slack as I stared out the window through the rain. "Did you see those fire hydrants?"

"They're all painted like that," he said wearily. "Some of them are Disney characters. They've got Pluto, Snow White. The one outside my parents' house is supposed to be the Flying Nun."

"How do you make a fire hydrant look like a nun?"

"You don't."

We drove past a scattering of modest houses and onto Plummer Avenue, passing Tim Hortons and The Bingo Palace, two buildings that assumed pride of place in New Waterford by dint of being newly constructed. The rest of the five-block promenade revealed a rickety old veteran's hall between some boarded up storefronts with FOR LEASE signs nailed to their doors. There was a pharmacy, Lawton's Drugs, which appeared to cater to the geriatric given the listing tower of Depends packages displayed in its window; a video store promoting *Dinosaur* with a cardboard cutout of a triceratops glaring at an idle handful of teenagers in windbreakers, who were smoking and shivering in the gloom; we passed a Pay-a-Dollar Store and Muise's Dairy and a tavern called Room with a Cue.

Calvin turned left onto King Street and pulled up in front of a little house, which was painted eggshell blue and ringed with a crowded assortment of lawn ornaments. When I opened the car door, it knocked into a fire hydrant with peering eyes and a black nun's habit. Her nose was the huge round snout where the water hose fits, which didn't look quite right. "Frannie, try not to get my mother started on the fire hydrant," Calvin said. "She'll never shut up."

Nearby, a Doberman pinscher howled in someone's yard, chained and neglected. The neon bucket of a Kentucky Fried Chicken outlet cast stripes of red and white light on the widewalk.

"So here we are," Calvin said glumly, easing out of the car and stretching his cramped legs.

I took a vigorous breath, trying to inhale the sea air; I could hear the Atlantic's low thunder a hundred yards down this street, beyond a handful of houses surrounded by sea grass. But all I could smell was coal, so acrid that it startled me.

"Why does it smell like that?" I asked.

"They still use coal to heat their houses."

"It can't be good for Lester?"

Calvin looked at the baby, still asleep in the car, his little mouth hanging open. "I'm not worried about him. I'm worried about you."

"Oh . . . no. Don't say that, Calvin, that's patronizing. I will be fine." I trotted up the path to the front door and rang the bell.

My son's grandmother threw open the door, clutched my head to her breast, and screamed, "I love you, I love you, I love you! Oh my God!" and then burst into tears. Under the circumstances, offering my hand for a shake seemed unnecessary. I hugged her. Big loving smile. Best behavior. "Hello, Mrs. Puddie, it's so nice to meet you."

She was an absolute vision of terrycloth. A pink terrycloth bathrobe billowed over yellow terrycloth stretch pants and matching top, while her feet flapped about in purple terrycloth slippers. She was round as a ball. I'd never seen anything like it. It was as if someone had upholstered a bean-bag chair in towels.

"Oh my God," she sobbed, wringing her plump hands, "we thought he was gay! We had no hope for him atall! Come in, dear, come in, I hope you didn't have too much trouble on the road."

She ushered me into a little sitting room stuffed with knickknacks, like a magpie's den. There were Beanie Babies and needlepoint cushions and Red Rose Tea figurines and Virgin Mary statues and doilies. Lots of doilies, really, a kind of infestation of doilies spreading like a fungus on every surface. The room was dominated by two huge easy chairs facing a TV, each of which was draped with three or four doilies. Bernice followed my gaze. "Those are doilies, dear. I make them with my Doodle-loom."

"They're lovely," I said.

"Do you use Doodle-looms in Toronto?" She peered at me anxiously through her big square glasses, her eyes watery and pale. "I use a Doodle-loom with my Knit-Wit kit, but Shirley says in Toronto they favor something else, I don't recall the name. She says they're too stuck-up for Knit-Wit. How many appliances have you got, dear?"

"Ten," I offered, gamely switching gears, keeping my hands clasped like a schoolgirl.

"Does that include your washer and dryer?" She stood a few inches away and studied me almost tremulously, as if she were about to burst into tears again.

"Um . . . yes, a washer and a dryer," I replied airily, "and a microwave oven, and a stove and—well, I don't know if a hairdryer counts . . ." I trailed off. She had gone through her teensy dining room and into the kitchen, and was waving at me to follow.

"The trip must have wore you out. Would you like a cuppa tea?" My breasts were pricking, of all things. Lester needed to be fed. I realized that one of the first things I was going to have to do in front of this woman, other than tally entirely invented appliances, was whip out my breasts. Astonishingly, she beat me to it.

"Did Stanley tell you I got cancer?" she asked.

"No, I'm so sorry, I didn't know that. I haven't actually spoken to Stanley."

"Oh, I get them mixed up," she fretted. "I meant Calvin. Stanley's my husband. I had cancer all over my middle, oh, it was awful dear. Oh my God." All at once, she yanked up her terrycloth top as unselfconsciously as a child. Her breasts were absent, and in their stead was a tangle of white scar tissue. In my surprise, I stammered out something so solicitous and nonsensical that it might not even have been in English.

She paid no attention. "Oh, they made a right mess of me," she lamented. "They hacked me to pieces. And it didn't do no good. Look!" She rolled up the sleeve of her bathrobe to reveal a pale and flabby arm covered in marble-size bumps. "I got arm cancer."

"Oh dear," I said.

"I was up at the Regional last week to get more cancer medicine, dear, I keep running out. They got me taking so many pills I get confused. I think I got the cancer medicine mixed up with my Tums."

At this, she let loose a veritable torrent of commentary about doctors' appointments and blood-pressure pills and pharmacy bills and whether or not to eat meat pies when your "stomach's not too good," and what Shirley said and what Stanley said and how the cancer medicine made her legs blow up like balloons. And then she looped around and began reiterating all this information as if she hadn't just said it.

"What's all this, Bernice?" boomed a voice from the living room. "Boring her senseless with Knit-Wit, are you?" Calvin's father was descending a short staircase and eyeballing me with a welcoming grin. I walked forward to meet him. He was tall and stooped, with sleek gray hair and a long, angular face, his spectacles as thickly lensed as his wife's. A plaid shirt hung loosely from his bony shoulders, tucked neatly into thin brown slacks.

"Good to see you," he said. "You're a fine-looking woman. We thought Calvin was gay. Where's my grandson?"

"He's asleep in the car, and Calvin just went to the corner store," I explained. "But actually I need to feed him, so . . ."

"Nancy, you bring in the baby," Bernice said to me, "and I'll make you tea and introduce you to Shirley and Dougal. I promised I'd call them as soon as you came. They bought some presents for the little one, bless their hearts."

Thus I found myself, within half an hour, reclining precariously in an easy chair with my breasts exposed to Calvin's entire Clan Calum Ruadh, all of whom were watching me like a brand-new TV show, and none of whom were epic.

"He's gotta set o' lungs on him, eh, Nancy?" said Shirley, when I shifted Lester from one breast to the other, prompting him to bawl frantically until he saw where he was headed.

"Oh, it's Frannie, actually," I said, terribly embarrassed, as if I'd deliberately misled them.

"Hah!" laughed Shirley. "One of these days I swear Bernice is going to get her own name wrong, eh Stanley?" Mr. Puddie chuckled.

Shirley was Bernice's sister. She was wearing identical yellow terrycloth stretch pants. Calvin later explained that this was because Shirley and Bernice shopped together compulsively at the Cotton Ginny in the Mayflower

Mall. But if Bernice was as plump as a hedgehog, Shirley was lean, and looked frazzled by alcohol. Her hair was frizzed from a lifetime of perms and her face was wrinkly and pallid. Shirley's husband, Dougal, was squat and square-jawed. He clapped his close-set eyes on me with unabashed curiosity.

"No use for the bottle then, eh?" he asked. Bottle was pronounced bawt'l, the Cape Breton accent being somewhat like North Dakota's and then something unto itself, with *car* being "care" and *Aladdin,* "alaad'n."

"Well," I stammered, flushing, "I'll feed him this way for a while, but you know . . ." I smiled brightly and covered my breast with a doily.

"You and Stanley are cousins?" I ventured into the ensuing silence, trying to remember what Calvin had told me.

"We're all cousins," said Dougal. The four of them nodded at me in unison.

"Me and Stanley are cousins," Bernice added. "That's why we got the same eyes." I shot a wild, alarmed look at Calvin but he was staring studiously at the television set, as if he'd always been interested in the Shopping Channel, had always been there, on that sofa, eyeballing Zyrcon rings.

When Calvin brought Lester in from the car, his mother had covered him with kisses and then followed him around the house dogging him with anxious queries:

"Do you need socks, Stan? Would you like some meat pie with homemade relish? Do you need me to launder your socks? Is that light too bright for the baby? Should I make a set of house keys for you and Nancy? In case Daddy and I have to go to the hospital when you're out for a walk? Does the baby need some Pablum, cause I got Instant Oatmeal but I don't know if that's all right, do you think he'd choke on the peach bits, should I get proper Pablum? Does the baby need socks?"

Calvin uttered taciturn replies: "Yes, no, yes, no, we're fine, don't worry about it, Mum," evading her while he did his few chores, storing the suitcase beside the sofa, rinsing off Lester's pacifier, changing his shirt in the bathroom, until there was nothing left to do and he was effectively cornered, whereupon she reiterated the torrent she'd poured out to me about doctors and cancer pills and Shirley, and there was nothing for Calvin to do but settle tensely on the couch and turn his head to the TV.

It came to me that this was why he was such a quiet man, because he grew up in a household where opening his mouth threatened to start a conversation.

"Well, we picked up a few things for the little one," said Shirley, approaching me with a pile of parcels. "You go on and open them and I'll take the baby." She reached for Lester with her lit-up smile and I handed him over. He stared at Shirley with interest. He was too little to feel anxiety. The waitresses had virtually kidnapped him at the diner of the Motel Guy Motel in Moncton, while Calvin and I finished our fish and chips. We saw him contemplating the fake ferns as his small round head bobbed above the shoulder of a waitress named Yolande, and then he vanished with her into the kitchen for a good fifteen minutes. Now Shirley and Bernice blathered happily at him while I opened their presents: two yellow terrycloth sleepers, a woolen toque with bunny ears, a Smurf, and a couple of afghans.

"Stanley made one of 'em," said Bernice. "He borrowed my Doodle-Loom."

Stanley, who had been reclining in his easy chair, smiled and winked at me. "I do the Knit-Wit from time to time," he said. "Keeps me nimble."

"That's extremely kind of you," I said. It was so unexpected and sweet, to think of this gruff and lanky old miner working on a Doodle-Loom. As if to ward off my expression of warmth, Stan got up and punched Dougal in the shoulder. "Git off yer carcass, old-timer, we got a Tarabish table waitin'."

That was a favorite card game in Cape Breton, I came to learn. His father and uncle played at the veteran's hall while Shirley and Bernice went to bingo.

"See you at supper, Frannie," he added. "Bernice done up a ham."

Let Us Talk Now of Appliances

At five o'clock, Bernice loaded her doily-festooned dining table with plates of maple ham, mashed turnips, boiled cauliflower, shredded beef pie, cole slaw, slices of Wonder Bread, and cracked white bowls filled with homemade condiments. She offered me some Diet Double Fudge Soda or, alternatively, tea. I said water would be fine. After everyone's needs got sorted out and we settled in to eat, the conversation turned to appliances.

"Does the baby have any appliances, Nancy?" Bernice turned to me with her watery gaze.

"Um, I'm not sure what you mean. Like a . . . like my breast pump? Or—"

"I saw a baby masher on sale at Wal-Mart," she explained. "Stanley." Bernice slapped at her husband's arm. "What was that thing called, remember we saw it last weekend and we thought maybe Calvin and Nancy could use one like that? That thing on sale?"

"You're full of old rope, Bernice," Stan said scornfully, wiping his mouth with a napkin. "There's no appliance that mashes babies. What are you on about?"

"For *food*, you old fool," Bernice said. "Don't you recall that appliance that mashes up baby food, like turnips and potatoes and such?"

"You mean the baby grinder," Stan corrected.

"That was it, baby grinder. You got one of those, Nancy?"

"Mum," Calvin interrupted, "her name isn't Nancy. It's Fran. Nancy's your cousin in Montreal. Can you try to remember to call her Fran, please?"

"Oh, I'm getting all mixed up again," she said ruefully. "But it isn't my cousin I keep thinking of, Calvin, it's my girlfriend in Germany. Fran is the spittin' image of her, don't you think, Stan?"

"When were you in Germany?" I asked, surprised.

"After the war, hon. Stanley stayed on working for the military after the war."

"Oh sure," said Stan. "We were there until 1949. After the war ended I brought Bernice over. Kept myself out of the mines that way."

"What was the war like for you?" I asked, quickening to a subject that I could at least gain some traction on.

"Oh, it was something else," he said affably, concentrating on his food. "You know. Saw my own brother blown up by a shell. We were just finished playing bridge. We had this game set up in the trenches. Four of us playing off and on, you know, when the action was quiet. He said, 'See you later, Stan,' and off he goes, couple of steps, and that was it. End of my brother." He recounted this so mildly that I found my hand frozen with the fork halfway to my mouth.

Over the next few days, I prodded him for stories, which he was always content to relay. It became our preferred conversation subject at the table, not surprisingly, since there turned out to be nothing else. He played affectionately with Lester, but didn't ask about him. Or about us. Neither of them evinced the slightest interest in our lives.

I kept waiting for Mrs. Puddie to ask Calvin substantive questions like "How are you?" or "Do you have a job?" But she never did; she remained on the plane of immediacy, like a child. "Were you comfortable on the pull-out bed, dear? Do you want me to bring down the electric blanket? Do you have enough socks?"

Was she truly that incurious about her only son? Or was she afraid of the answers? Or unable to find the language, to know what to ask? Calvin shrugged helplessly when I put this to him. We were strolling along Plummer Avenue with Lester in his carriage, wincing at the view, which featured stoned adolescents and lonely tethered dogs.

"She's always been like that," he said simply. "Ever since I can remember. She barely registered the fact that I moved to New York."

"But why?" I persisted. "She seems to love you to death, why doesn't she want to know about your life?"

We passed by the Tim Hortons. A crowd had gathered in the parking lot and was jostling to get in the door. Word had gone around that an apparition of the Virgin Mary had materialized in the vinyl countertop near the cash register. The cashier thought it was a coffee spill and tried to clean it up, but it remained there as a stubborn brown smudge.

"Holy jumpin', it's the Madonna!" the cashier concluded, according to Bernice. Then everybody started driving over, from Sydney and Glace Bay and the Mi'k-maq reserve, ambling through the door in their parkas to kiss the counter stain and bless themselves before buying a bucket of Tim-Bits.

"She doesn't want to know about my life," Calvin said irritably, "because my life isn't here in Cape Breton. That's the way it is. You're either on the island, or your outline blurs and they lose sight of you in the fog that covers the rest of the planet. That's the way it is."

"Sort of like Manhattan," I mused. "I guess there are advantages. You could have become Robert Mapplethorpe and they wouldn't have noticed."

He leaned forward and adjusted Lester's bunny-ears hat, which had slid down over his eyes. I watched him, watched his tenderness, and wondered suddenly if it made him lonely, to be part of a family that didn't want to know what made him tick, what gave him joy.

True Love at Last

I decided that I had to find a way to connect with Calvin's parents—surely there was a way—so I impulsively paid a visit to the video store. I had the idea that I'd watch *Saving Private Ryan* with his dad—why not?—and draw out more feelings, more memories, the shape of his life. After a supper of baked haddock and macaroni, our movie viewing amidst the doilies went something like this:

Sound of bullets hissing through the air. Men crying out. Vomiting. Shells exploding. Dismembered limbs whizzing by.
TOM HANKS: Move, men, move.
DYING SOLDIER: Mommy . . .
ME (gently): Does this . . . does this ring true for you, Mr. Puddie?
STAN (*after a contemplative pause):* Well, I was in It'ly. Not Normandy, but—

PATRICIA PEARSON

BERNICE: They painted the fire hydrant over on Queen Street as Mrs. Doubtfire. Did I tell you already? It looks just as mad as the nun. Me and Shirley warned them, you can't get around that round nozzle thing on the hydrant, it's gonna make your females look like fat pigs with snouts. Smurfs are fine, but they got such a job with these other ones, lord love us. Nancy, did I show you my apple dolls?

After three days in New Waterford, I took to hiding in the basement. Not on purpose, at first, but just going down to check on Lester's laundry, or to use the little bathroom, or sift through family pictures. After awhile, I took to reading down there on a rickety, three-legged stool beside the freezer. Shirley, it turned out, had a vast collection of romance novels, which she and Bernice had stored in the basement in anticipation of a summer yard sale. At her urging, I got immersed in what was said to be the best of the lot, *I Thee Wed*, by someone named Amanda Quick. The setting was England in, like, the past, when aristocrats wore ball gowns. The heroine: fiery, red-haired Emma Greyson, a paid lady's companion with such a flair for taking umbrage that she would probably be classified as having borderline personality disorder in modern England. The hero: Edison Stokes, icy, wealthy, and hung like a bison.

I read about half of it, unconsciously editing out whole paragraphs as I went along, and finally slapped it down on my knee. Romance novels! What a strange breed of fiction. No other genre devotes itself exclusively to exploiting reader sexual frustrations in such a long-winded manner. Porn mags cater to desire, of course, but they wouldn't remotely claim to hold your attention for more than one page. What are the plot lines in *Playboy?* Protagonist: Debbi, twenty-one, loves sweating and pouting. The end.

Romance novels traffic in sexual fantasy by actually dragging you through plots. After perusing the dust jackets on Shirley's collection I determined that the plots of romance novels vary in the following ways: name of heroine, location of love affair, synonym for penis. Otherwise, they appear to subscribe to fixed principles: Man and woman must meet within first five pages; woman must be proud, smart, and scrappy; man must be aloof, emotionally inarticulate, and insulting; they must hate each other; both must be stunning; they must get embroiled against their wishes; they must boink like rabbits; they must glide down the aisle.

The basic idea is that a woman's sexual fantasy is to find a gorgeous man with whom she can fight and screw like an alley cat, pretty much into infinity. You know, like Elizabeth Taylor and Richard Burton—as opposed to their characters in *Who's Afraid of Virginia Woolf?* whose bickering would be the logical conclusion to all romance novel plots if their trajectory continued beyond the altar.

"Gimme another scotch, you insufferable bitch."

"Get it yourself, you arrogant slob!"

Women pine for sexual drama. Certainly I do. I want to have lived Taylor's life on the set of *Cleopatra*. I want to be fickle and unstable and immature, so that men of elegance will clutch me, overcome with desire. If only I had the guts to storm off on my lover the second he turned on the hockey game, provoking him to seethe in cold fury, helplessly admiring my spirit, then press his searching mouth to my lips. Instead of not noticing.

I quoted the ending of one of these novels to Calvin:

"He nuzzled her neck, and his thumbs moved up to stroke beneath the swell of her breasts. 'I am reputed to be the wealthiest man in England, but I can see you are determined to beggar me before you are done.'

"Her sultry laugh rang out happily. 'I shall certainly try my very best, you black devil.' "

The end.

I tried ringing out a happy, sultry laugh of my own, and Calvin asked me if I was all right before padding into the kitchen to rinse out some spit bibs.

Is it, or is it not, a crisis to have a world without windows and walls and a roof, to not have made love to your partner for months, to be divested of the fantasies that spur you?

Is it? Or not?

Bingo Brain

In retrospect, it could be argued that anxiety began to snake through me on the day we arrived in New Waterford. But it didn't start to free-float, as my mother would say, until that night, when we retired to our pullout couch and I developed the fear that the house was going to fall over. It was just a passing notion at first, as I tossed and turned beside Calvin beneath our Hudson Bay blanket. Something along the lines of: *This house is really very small, I wonder how it fares in a wind storm?* I just got to thinking about that, how a gale might thunder in from the Atlantic, for example, and what would keep the house standing, given that it appeared to be constructed entirely of aluminum siding.

Would it not, in fact, blow away? Or maybe it wouldn't, but maybe all the garden gnomes on the street would get ripped out of the grass and become a crowd of projectiles hurtling into the wall. That could definitely happen. I thought about it for a while. Then a new notion struck me. Lester could blow away. We could be walking along the bluff like we did yesterday when we saw that rotting seal carcass, and the wind would push his carriage over the sloping rock face so that it rattled and bounded helplessly down like the carriage on the Odessa staircase in the *Battleship Potemkin*.

My heart began to thud. I listened for the wind, which was ceaseless in New Waterford, keeping my hair in a permanent tangle. I could hear its low moan, and the distant tinkle of wind chimes, the desperate barking of the yard dogs.

What if the sound of the wind disguised something else, I suddenly wondered, like the low chuff-chuffing of a moose? What if a moose came into the garden and . . . *What if the moose was rabid?* It might very plausibly kick in the front door, which was a foot from my head.

"Calvin, wake up."

"Huh?"

"Are there any moose in New Waterford?"

"Why?" He opened one eye and looked at me.

"What if there's a moose in the yard?"

"Then hopefully it will step on my mother's Little Black Sambo statue and crush it to dust." The eye fluttered shut.

"Calvin, I'm serious."

"Go to sleep, Frannie. I promise there's nothing large in the yard."

He, himself, fell back to sleep instantly. How bitterly I

envied him, that he could breathe so deeply and dream so pleasantly while I remained vigilant on his and Lester's behalf, on guard against nocturnal beasties.

The thing about an anxiety attack is that whatever makes you anxious in the first place—like homelessness, career implosion, motherhood, romantic crisis, getting fat, and Mrs. Puddie—quickly gets lost in a stampede of panicked fantasies about wind, Doberman pinschers, parka-clad hooligans, meat pie botulism, flying garden gnomes, rabid moose, and oversalted infants: a veritable parade of catastrophic scenarios fashioned from the material at hand. I had forgotten all about the insidious creep-up of anxiety, how you don't realize that you're being irrational for the longest time. Thus it was that two nights after watching *Saving Private Ryan*, I genuinely thought I was having a heart attack in the Bingo Palace.

The whole fiasco began when Bernice and Shirley cajoled me into accompanying them to their weekly game, leaving three generations of Puddie male at home to watch the Stanley Cup play-offs while snacking, respectively, on meusli muffins, Doritos, and Pablum.

"Have you got the markers, Shirley?" Bernice worried. They were packing an equipment bag of sorts, which included a dozen fat bingo blotters to stamp their sheets with, two prized figurines for good luck, a tin of caramel squares, and a thermos of tea.

"I got new ones that don't leak so much," said Shirley. She was weaving a little as they bustled about the house. She'd had too many rye and Cokes with supper. I had to be home to breast-feed by ten and felt, in that sense, rather like Cinderella going to the ball. That little frisson of tension amplified almost immediately when we clambered into Shirley's Ford Pinto and she roared out of the driveway and promptly ran over a cat.

"Oh, for the love of God," said Bernice, peering apprehensively out the passenger side window for signs of roadkill.

"I didn't hit it square-on," said Shirley, craning out her own window. "It took a bit of a blow, that's all. Probably scampered off already."

I clutched the door handle and tried to breathe deeply as Shirley stepped on the gas, lurched, and came to a jolting stop again at Plummer Avenue. From here it was only three blocks, which she covered successfully, still arguing with Bernice about the fate of the cat, one opting for minimal damage while the other fretfully presumed the worst. Then, having parked beside Muise's Dairy, the pair of them pushed me excitedly through the doors of the Bingo Palace and into a hot, bright, gymnasium-sized room.

It was crowded with long, bare tables, which were dotted with tin-foil ashtrays. Chairs were scraping back, ladies of all ages were taking their favorite places, setting out their Cokes and coffees and lucky totems and gabbling about the prizes. At the back of the room on a stage, a gray-haired man with lambchop sideburns and a face made ruddy from liquor was sitting with his chin in his hand, wearily scanning the room, waiting for the forty or fifty players to assemble. When the hall settled down, dozens of moon faces turned to the caller expectantly and he leaned into a microphone and began.

"B-fifty-two."

There was a scattered sound of sheets being marked, like the first pops of corn in a pan.

"Got it, got it," Shirley muttered, taking a quick swig of Coke without peeling her eyes away from her six cards. Bernice did not have it, and looked fleetingly for-lorn, as if Shirley always got ahead of her like this, had all the breaks.

"N-sixteen," intoned the gray-haired man, and the hall replied with a rapid smattering of thuds.

"G-one."

My hand hovered in the air, clutching my marker far too tightly. I was breaking into a sweat, casting my eyes anxiously all over my cards for the requisite numbers and letters, as if speed-reading an ophthalmologist's chart. I couldn't seem to concentrate. Two thoughts kept whizzing around in my head as distractingly as moths. One, flitting across the surface of my consciousness, was that I really should have followed up on that date with the guy in New York whose parents were Broadway composers, because maybe he was kind of dull, but was he really that dull?

And the other one, more pressing, was: *What if I actually have to yell Bingo?*

"O-twenty-nine," the man on the dais called gruffly.

Impatient with my slow-witted approach to the cards, Shirley reached over and stamped some squares for me.

"I-eighteen."

She did mine again. I followed suit politely, jabbing at the remaining square marked I-eighteen and smiling at her apologetically. "Guess it takes practice."

"B-five."

"O-twelve."

To my horror, the blots of purple ink were beginning to line up on one of my cards. My breathing got shallow. I tried to inhale more deeply, but the air, as such, had been replaced by Player's Light cigarette smoke with undertones of hairspray and sweat. It flew through my mind that I was going to sustain brain damage from hazardous waste exposure and perish before Lester hit grade three.

"O-ten."

"Awwwk," screeched Shirley, stamping my card and gesticulating excitedly at her sister. "She got it, Bernice, she got it!" The sisters waited a beat and when I said nothing, Bernice leaned over and lightly shook my elbow. "You got bingo, dear, you got to shout it out."

A wave of heat washed through me. I felt flickers of pain in my chest, as if the heat had ignited a fire in my heart, which was as tight and dense as coal. "Bingo," I whispered.

Shirley and Bernice looked astonished. They stared frantically back and forth between me and the caller, who plodded on in his gruff voice, unaware that anyone had triumphed and could now claim the porcelain snowman toilet-roll dispenser.

"No-thirty-six."

"Say it louder, Frannie, by Jesus," snapped Shirley.

"Bingo," I hollered, and fifty heads swiveled to ogle

the lucky winner. I clutched my chest and tried to breathe. It came to me that I was having a heart attack, and that I should probably point that out to someone.

"I think I'm having a heart attack," I said.

"I beg your pardon, dear?" asked Bernice.

"I think . . . I'm sorry. I need to see a doctor."

It took her a moment to wrap her mind around what I was saying, and then, all at once, she got the idea and began tearing at her hair. "Lord in heaven, Nancy's having a coronary!" She waved at Shirley, who had scooted off, doing celebratory little butt wags, to collect the prize on my behalf.

"Shirley, Shirley," called Bernice, "get back here, where's Al got to? Nancy's taken sick!"

Al, another cousin, was an off-duty ambulance driver who fancied Bingo over Tarabish and was hanging about in the hall. Duly summoned by a pair of women squawking like peacocks, the bald and rake-thin Al rushed to my side and took my arm gently, "All right, dear, it's all right," leading me through the watching crowd with Shirley and Bernice following behind.

In a flash, the three of them had whisked me up the street to the New Waterford Hospital, which Bernice knew intimately, given her infrequent cancer treatments interspersed—according to Stanley—with frequent bouts of hypochondria. As we entered the crowded emergency room she called out for "Doris" and "Henry," like we'd rushed into the family kitchen. Familiarity bred contempt. After a quick look at Bernice and then at me, Dr. Doris McKeen triaged my case behind a young man who'd almost cut his head off with a chainsaw—"Damn fool," his father kept muttering—and a woman who'd driven headlong into the brick wall of Room with a Cue. Also ahead of me was a pensioner rasping and hacking with pneumonia, a Mi'k-maq fellow who'd fallen through the spring ice and sat shivering violently in his wet plaid wool jacket, a boy whose foot had been run over by a skidoo, a man with a migraine, a woman with a hangnail, and someone suffering from ennui.

Dr. McKeen apparently knew at a glance what was now, slowly, occurring to me, as I sat on my pale-blue scalloped chair beside Bernice.

"You know," I finally allowed to Bernice, "I don't think I'm having a heart attack. Because we've been sitting here for forty-five minutes and I'm just thinking that a heart attack would have come and gone by now and I'd be dead."

"You can't know," Bernice argued. "These doctors don't care if you're dyin'—they still go off on their coffee breaks and talkin' on the phone, oh, it's somethin' else here, I'm telling you. Maybe you got a different sickness, though. Asthma, maybe. Or cancer."

The hair on the back of my neck rose and I began hyperventilating.

Shirley grew bored of the stalled drama and left to debrief Calvin. Bernice wouldn't hear of going home. She was loyal to me, and kind. The ER was also her equivalent of a Southern lady's front porch, from whence she kept tabs on her neighbors. She sat beside me with her plump legs crossed at the ankles, dipping a hand every now and then into the Lays potato chips bag she extracted from a vending machine, and leaning over to whisper congenial anecdotes into my ear about the unfortunate souls who staggered in.

Eventually, I was blessed by the full attention of Dr. McKeen.

"You're suffering from anxiety, Ms. Mackenzie," she said, warmly squeezing my shoulders. She was a tall woman with light blue eyes and laugh lines, a fringe of brown bangs, and a small nose smattered with freckles. She wasn't much older than me.

"You're not from here," she added, checking me again with the stethoscope, "so what are you doing with Bernice, of aa'l people? You're not getting married, are you?" She stepped back. "You came here with Bernice's son. Would that be causing the panic?" She was smiling so wryly and sympathetically that I wanted to follow her home. I explained about Calvin and Lester, and how I thought I'd been living in New York, but then I was in Toronto, and . . . it sounded as disjointed as the plot of a dream.

"Oh my," murmured Dr. McKeen, and: "What a bumpy road." She gently pressed a prescription for Xanax into my palm, and then invited Calvin and me to dinner, to talk about Bernice. "I wouldn't think she's articulated her condition very clearly?"

I shook my head. "She says she has arm cancer."

"All right then," Dr. McKeen scribbled down her address, then drew back the green curtain surrounding my bed and headed off. "You come on over this weekend and we'll taa'lk."

"What do I have to do to keep you out of trouble?" Calvin asked, having walked up the hill to the hospital, leaving Lester to sleep in his father's lap. He put his arm around me and escorted me out through the doors to the misty darkness. His mother was waiting, clutching her purse and her Bingo bits and pieces. "One minute you're locked in the basement with Penny's thoughts and the next thing I know, you've got Bingo Brain."

"That was certainly not a one-minute time span."

"You're right. Other shit happened too. We're building a history, Frannie, a little book of stories for the grand-kids."

A Brief Note About the
Shoplifting Habits of Infants

From the knee-high vantage point of his stroller, Lester had grown adept at removing objects from the shelves of stores, which I invariably discovered when we'd progressed several hundred yards down the street. When I glanced into his lap, I would notice a gnawed peach, for instance, or a Britney Spears CD. Calvin tried to encourage Lester to steal useful things, like Pampers. But of course, we couldn't be complicit in the act. We had to just hope he had grabbed something good. It was like leaving a party with a loot bag.

The day after my anxiety attack, I went to Lawton's Drugstore to fill out my prescription for Xanax and buy cans of Similac, while Lester accumulated a box of toothpicks, some Ex-Lax, and a light bulb, which he serenely tossed out of his stroller just as I was turning into the Puddies' driveway. It exploded with a pop on the gravel.

His grandfather, who was washing his rarely driven Lincoln, witnessed this small incident and laughed appreciatively.

"He takes after my side of the family," Stan said. "Sure he does." He reached down and gently lifted Lester up to cradle him in the crook of his arm. "You're a Puddie, all right," he cooed into the face of his kin. "Sure you are."

I didn't wish to inquire about theft through the generations. I just stood there marveling at the small revelation that Lester was a child in the world, bringing love to a stranger from whom he descended.

What We Fear

"I'm flying on an airplane next month, and that just fills me with knee-buckling dread. I'm telling you. It scares me to death." Dr. McKeen offered this confession in her kitchen, where she was deep-frying strips of halibut while Calvin and I sat around her big oak table drinking beer. Lester was playing with some measuring spoons on the floor at my feet, babbling and making tinkling sounds.

"Listen to me, Frannie," Dr. McKeen continued, "you wouldn't believe what people are afraid of. I mentioned my fear of flying to a friend who works down in Halifax, and he said that he had a phobia of cotton batten. He said if he were locked in a small room filled neck-high with cotton balls, he would scream so uncontrollably that he might actually have a heart attack and die."

"Get outta town," said Calvin.

"I'm not making it up. Go on and ask my husband. He's been collecting people's phobias for a book."

Doris's husband was a huge, redheaded Irishman who smoked like Vaclev Havel and hobbled around on one leg, having lost the other to a rare bone cancer in his teens. He was loud and animated and loved to argue, having already picked a fight with Calvin about whether or not experimental jazz was a bunch of "unlistenable rot." Johnny raised hell for one of the environmental groups lobbying the government to clean up the toxic waste in Sydney Harbor. He appeared in the kitchen doorway and leaned against the frame.

"Go on, ask me," he said. "Ask me what people are afraid of. I've got a list." He fished around in his shirt pocket and tossed me a piece of paper covered in his big, boisterous handwriting. Herewith, the phobias of the descendants of Calum Rhuad Clan, two centuries after they came to the land of the trees:

Plastic bags floating on puddles, which must be avoided by crossing the street.

Loose buttons, which cause high alarm when spied on a table, and cannot be touched at any cost.

Vomit, which cannot be mentioned without risk of panic attack.

Honey, which obliges the sufferer to shower after contact.

Lizards, which cannot be named without upset.

Mirrors, which cannot be looked at under any circumstances.

Clowns, which deeply unsettle.

Eggs, which cannot be regarded sunnyside up on a plate.

Fingertips placed together hand to hand, or people who place other sharp objects, like pencils, end to end against their fingertips, reminding the sufferer of finger bones scraping together, and "scaring the hell out of me."

Balloons, which cannot be allowed at sufferer's children's birthday parties, much to sufferer's children's regret.

Johnny hobbled over to me and tapped the paper with his hand.

"I got these phobias from people who live out near the Tar Ponds, worst toxic waste site in Canada. We've got six-toed cats being born out there. Miscarriages, cancer, you name it. It's a stinking mess. And these people are afraid of balloons." He sat down. "People are afraid of stupid bullshit, that's what. They're never afraid of what's actually scary. Look at me." He gestured at his body. "I've got one leg and one lung. I should be afraid of cancer. But you know what I'm afraid of?"

Calvin and I shook our heads.

"Dandelions," he boomed. "Hitchcock could have made a horror movie with dandelions." He mimed a movie marquee: *"The Dandelions."* Then he shivered theatrically. "You think I'm joking, but I'm not. You could chase me right out of this house with a dandelion."

"You can't be serious," Calvin said.

"Oh no?" Johnny retorted. "What's your phobia, Calvin?"

Calvin shrugged and crossed his arms uncooperatively. "Don't have one."

261

"Yes you do," I interjected. "Calvin has a phobia of mayonnaise."

"It isn't a phobia," Calvin said disdainfully, but Johnny was already heaving himself up and heading for the fridge. He whipped out a jar of Hellmann's and waved it in Calvin's face.

"Arrrrgggghhhhhhhh!" shouted Calvin, leaning backward until he almost fell out of his chair. *"Get away from me with that shit."*

"I rest my case," said Johnny, returning the Hellmann's to the fridge.

"What case?" asked Calvin, thoroughly unnerved.

"Why are you afraid of condiments and not of your mother having cancer? Tell me that!" Johnny yelled, like a prosecutor cross-examining a witness.

Doris brought a platter of fish and chips to the table and held the back of her hand to her mouth, trying to calm down from laughing about the mayonnaise in order to say something serious.

"Bernice doesn't have cancer," she finally announced, looking at Calvin. "She hasn't had a recurrence since the radical mastectomy. She told Johnny she had cancer in her middle, last time she saw him at Sobey's. Your mother has some cysts. That's all. I think she's started to use the word *cancer* as a catchphrase for whatever ails her. Maybe she equates it with aging."

Calvin listened to this with keen interest. Then he leaned down and collected Lester, settling him on his knees and kissing him lightly on the head. "Hmm," he merely said.

I was extremely relieved by this news.

"Bernice has a tough old hide, don't let her fool you," Doris continued. "Sometimes I think her fear is a schtick. I don't know what to make of her. I know she's proud of you, Calvin. She's always telling us how she has this son down in Las Vegas who plays in an orchestra."

Calvin sighed.

"What are you afraid of, Frannie?" Johnny asked.

Oh, God. Where to begin. "Don't ask. It depends on what day it is."

"If it's Monday, it must be bingo," said Calvin.

Doris rose to offer second helpings of halibut.

"You know what?" she said. "Why don't you and Calvin leave the baby with us tomorrow night and take a little trip? It would be no trouble atall. He's a love, we'd keep him safe. He'd take a bawt'l more easily from me than you anyway, I'd think."

"Oh I couldn't do that. I'd be terrified," I said.

She looked at me and smiled, her wonderful blue eyes twinkling. "You're terrified of everything right now, anyway. You've got nothing to lose."

What We Wish For

Not a good idea, attempting a romantic road trip when one of you is anxious and the other is depressed. It doesn't quite work out like the hijinks in a Hollywood movie. If you came to a gas station, you could rob it and then make passionate love in a motel room, except that one of you says "Why bother?" and the other one is cowering in the footwell.

Calvin had fallen into a funk about his mother, for it seemed to distress him more that she'd fashioned a personality trait out of cancer than that she was actually battling illness. Meanwhile, I—although fully berated by Johnny concerning the right and wrong things to fear—was struggling with the conviction that the car was going to explode.

Thus I popped a Xanax and Calvin despondently took the wheel, and we followed the Atlantic shoreline heading north toward the Cape Breton highlands, in a glum, spaced-out silence.

Calvin had an idea about where he wanted to go, having to do with a friend from high school who'd built his own place in the woods. But he wasn't exactly loquacious about our destination. We could have been driving to Buffalo, for all I knew.

Toward midday, the winding two-lane highway we were following grew rougher and more pitted, and the thick forest of birch and maple along either side became denser, so that the car was largely in shadow. Here and there, as we rounded a bend, we came upon a run-down house with a broken washing machine or rusted car in the yard, dogs standing about aimlessly on the edge of the road, MOOSE CROSSING signs, a faded billboard obscured by foliage, advertising the Eskasoni bingo hall. We had entered Mi'kmaq territory. The reserve stretched on for miles, yet barely impinged upon the wilderness, with only flashes of human poverty every hundred yards or so amidst the trees.

Presently we came upon a much wider clearing, which played host to the Eskasoni Trading Post, a combination diner, variety store, and gas station pushing back into a steep, wooded hillside. A large number of people were milling about in the parking area, kicking at the gravel with their hands jammed into the pockets of their lumber jackets, waiting their turn, apparently, to talk to a television crew. We decided to stop for lunch.

PLAYING HOUSE

As we walked past the camera crew, we caught a snatch of conversation between the journalist, a tall, skinny man in Birkenstocks deferentially holding a microphone, and a gentle-voiced Mi'kmaq with furrowed white eyebrows.

"The old one says right away: it's the work of the fairies," the Mi'kmaq was explaining as the mike bobbed in front of his face. "Had to be. There was nobody came into the barn. Who the heck was going to braid a horse's mane anyhow? It hadda be done by some spirits of some kind."

We hesitated, and then pushed through the screen door of the Trading Post. A middle-aged woman, square and still as a block of wood, was standing behind a stained counter. Everybody else was outside.

"You with those TV people?" the woman asked, unsmiling, as we headed uncertainly toward her.

"No," I said. "Why are they here?"

She tossed her head to the left, as if to indicate something over her shoulder. All we could see were stacks of cigarettes and a block-board menu with letters missing, so that hot dogs were "hot do s" and beef burgers were "bee burg s."

"They come up to talk about the little people that lives in the hill up there," she explained.

"What little people?" I asked, confused.

"Fairies." Beyond that brief head toss, she hadn't moved a muscle. She seemed neither hostile nor friendly. She watched us impassively.

"Are you serving lunch?" I asked, feeling like it was the rudest question in the world.

She nodded, and gestured faintly at the counter. We sat down on the worn stools and ordered two bee burgs and some coffee. She went about her business quietly then, while I spun back and forth on my stool, and Calvin glanced curiously about the room. The only sound was the sizzle of grease on the grill.

Suddenly, the woman made an announcement. "They sit around makin' braids, that's what they do mostly."

"I beg your pardon?"

She wiped her gnarled hands on her white chef's apron and slid two plates toward us. "They take three or four straws. What they do is make a braid. Just sitting down, something to do. Making braids. I seen it a couple a times."

That afternoon, driving through the woods of Eskasoni, I thought about how wonderful it must be to believe in fairies, just like that. To know, for a fact, that you shared the world with supernatural creatures, that life was larger and more mysterious than science admitted, and humans were not in control.

"There is nothing to fear but fear itself," I said to Calvin.

"Right."

Half an hour later I felt compelled to add: "If we hit a moose, it would decapitate us, and Lester would be an orphan."

"True."

After another twenty minutes out came this observation: "Supposing there was an Ice Age, because some climatologists now think that's a plausible effect of global warming, you know. That the glaciers will melt and cool down the oceans. And some of them think it could happen very fast."

Silence.

"Well, it's a bit of a disaster, don't you think? What am I supposed to feed Lester if there's an Ice Age? Thawed tundra mulch?"

"Why don't we cross that bridge when we drive off of it."

And, finally: "Calvin, stop the car. I have to go to the bathroom."

"Fine."

He pulled over onto the dirt shoulder beneath a towering fir tree. The twilit air was perfectly windless, and deeply quiet. I stepped out of the car and crept into the undergrowth, batting at clouds of black flies and tangled brambles, shooting anxious glances every which way lest I be caught off guard by movement in the violet shadows. I squatted, coaxed down my jeans, began to pee, and then heard a sound. A rustle. The crack of a twig. A breathing sound. A snuffle or a sigh. I held my pee back and froze. I could hear my blood whoosh-whooshing in my ears. Another twig broke, closer this time. And then I saw it. A transparent darkness to my left, a shape but not discernible, a smell that I couldn't identify. A wavering presence. I shot out of the woods like a malfunctioning rocket with my pants around my shins. *"Drive,* Calvin, *drive!"*

He looked at me quizzically for a moment, and then obediently pulled off the shoulder and cruised down the road.

"I saw a fairy!" I shouted.

"You did not."

"I *did.*"

"Was it braiding straws at you?"

"I don't know what it was doing. It was studying me." I glanced in the rearview, suffused, still, with terror.

"Never get off the boat," Calvin remarked dryly.

Full of adrenaline, I rounded on him, twisting sideways in spite of my seat belt. "What is it with you? You're so mean! I *saw* a fucking *fairy.* I don't have a fairy phobia. I've never thought about fairies. I don't sit around going, 'oh no, a fairy.' It's not like you, going into the woods and running into a jar of Hellmann's." I banged my head against the headrest. "I need a drink."

"I'm sorry," he offered, shifting to sympathy. "Maybe you saw a fairy. But then you shouldn't be scared, you should feel blessed. I grew up here, and only ever saw garden gnomes."

It was hard to tell with Calvin, whether he was ever serious, whether the undercurrent of longing was there beneath the bluff, but maybe I detected a note of wistfulness. A desire to unveil the magic of Cape Breton for me, rather than feel only shame. His refusal to be solicitous of me, to offer up instead the gift of levity, had become so comforting. It only now struck me, in this moment, that I was letting him hide behind flippancy himself. I reached over to hold his hand. He caressed my fingers. "We'll be all right," he said quietly.

"How do you know?" I asked.

"I know."

We drove on through the darkness.

What We Live For

"Ah," he said at last, as our headlights illuminated a little sign on the side of the highway. "Lochend." He turned sharply to the right and juddered down a dirt road.

"Where are we going?" I asked.

"My Rivendel," he said. And for the first time all day, he looked truly pleased. Glimpses of light ahead cohered, at last, into the vivid picture of a house. Beyond it, a lake glimmered in the moonlight. We rolled to a stop.

The house appeared to be constructed of floor-to-ceiling glass windows set into the unpainted pinewood. A deck wrapped all around the rambling structure, with Adirondack chairs facing toward the lake. Amber light poured out of the windows and mingled with the cooler white light of the May moon.

"Calvin Puddie, where the hell did you come from,

you fat bastard?" An impossibly tall man with shaggy dark hair came down from the porch steps and across the rough drive to peer into our car window, his dark eyes shining in amusement. He wore a worn-out gray T-shirt, and dangled a beer bottle from one hand, with his thumb looped into his jeans pocket.

"Allistair Campbell," said Calvin, grinning. Then he turned to me. "This is the guy I told you about who threatened to run me over with his Pontiac if I didn't get out of New Waterford and study music." He leaned farther out of the car.

"Allistair, may I introduce Frannie Mackenzie, the love of my life, who just saw a fairy."

Allistair craned his neck to take me in, in my corner of the car. He nodded. "Fairies, man. They keep diggin' up my pot plant bulbs."

"It might have been a raccoon," I said, embarrassed.

"Welcome to Lochend, Frannie." He looked at Calvin. "I guess you're aiming for a slumber party, given the hour."

"I brought my dinosaur pajamas," Calvin said.

"Good man," replied Allistair.

We got out of the car and followed our host into his house.

There were no walls, except one, there to hold up the staircase. The rest of the space was open, divided only by its furniture into a kitchen, a dining room, and a living room, all of pine. Half a dozen people lounged about on dilapidated bits of furniture, resting instruments on their laps. Fiddles, flutes, guitars, an accordion. Everywhere a great deal of beer.

"Silly Puddie!" they hollered, as we walked into their midst. "You stupid sonofabitch! Droppin' in from nowhere!"

"By Jesus, Calvin, we thought we got rid o' ya."

Much hugging and back-slapping. A ponytailed guy who introduced himself as Craig offered us the dregs from a bowl of potato chips. "There's tons more, if you're hungry," he added. "Just poke your heads in the cupboard."

Allistair handed me a beer, patted my head. I was a good eighteen inches shorter. What did the top of my head look like? I suddenly wondered. The question crosses your mind, when you're feeling self-conscious in a room full of tall, braying men. We settled onto a low, springy couch and Calvin and his old high-school friends—which is what they were, for the most part—caught up on the news. A fellow named Doug in horn-rimmed glasses reported that he'd been playing in Ashley McIsaac's band. A possible career setback, however: He'd been looking after the famous fiddler's house near Baddeck and accidentally set it on fire, burning the entire three-story structure to the ground. Another friend, who was sprouting an unsuccessful goatee, reported that he was taking "dumb-assed fishermen" up and down the Margaree, trolling for salmon; he wintered on welfare and was making his way through the collected works of Noam Chomsky.

Calvin passed around a photograph of Lester.

"Shouldn't be legal, Puddie, you having offspring," said Doug.

"This is an earlier picture," I explained, after they'd all taken a gander at Lester in his Excersaucer. "He looks more like both of us now."

"For sure he's got Calvin's eyes," offered Allistair.

Yes, well, not surprisingly.

We told them about our trip to the Twilight Zone of infant colic, and the time that Calvin had to play marimba at a gig with Lester in a Snugli, because I was too tired to have him home with me. Egged on, we told more stories, about the Britney Spears CD and the time I locked him in the car. We were both holding the picture now, sitting knee to knee.

Allistair picked up a fiddle. "Grab some spoons, man," he said to Calvin, and they all joined in at once in an improvised session that was so sensuous and so lively, with foot-tapping, perspiration, singing and shouts, that I was left without presumption, without a doubt that the father of my child knew his joy. It lifted me up. His pleasure was a lifeline. I watched him clapping his spoons against his knee, tapping his foot on the pine boards, laughing in recognition when a new tune began, most of them rolicking Celtic and Acadian traditionals with the occasional, mocked pop song thrown in. His hair was damp and slicked back, his face bright. Aha. I knew it was the pot that made him look stuporous. Now he looked handsome. I thought of a quote my father was fond of.

"For a while I was at the center of my being, entirely within my element and in my light."

*   *   *

"What are you thinking?" he asked, still placid and sleepy. We were lying in a mess of blankets on the floor by the woodstove, our clothes in a heap, our bodies entwined in the deep quiet of dawn. I was staring at the darker whorls of wood within the amber walls of Allistair's house, at the way the window drew in the pale gray light; the meadow flowers that someone had placed in a jar. I could smell the wool of our blankets, the warm, sexy fragrance of our skin, the scent of smoke in the room, and of pine.

I was thinking about this book I had read as a girl, about a family pioneering in the forest somewhere or other, for whom small things brought such great pleasure, an orange for Christmas, a crisp dress ordered from a catalog. It made such a huge impression on me, I remember, how such little gifts could be treasured like that. It was as if I couldn't locate the sense of it in my own life, I couldn't see the gifts, I had to imagine them coming still.

Except that now I looked back on it, I perceived them so clearly, those small, significant joys: in the images in my books, and the hot dogs I ate on the beach, and the way my mother rhythmically squeezed my hand as I walked alongside her. It was this struggle, always, to take joy and make it present. To live, and stop planning to live.

Lester was teaching me to do that, but the lesson kept slipping away from me. I had to hold on to it, I wanted to hold on to it, now that I was safe within the solace that was Calvin's embrace.

"Earth to Frances." Calvin was waving his hand before my face. "What are you thinking?"

I rolled over to press myself into the hollow beneath his chin. "I'm thinking about what a gift you are. My someone to love."

"Pshaw." He threw the blanket over our heads. "Get outta town."

And Then We Lived
Happily Ever After

No, just kidding.

I can tell you that we went back to collect Lester from Doris and Johnny, and begged his forgiveness for the abandonment, even as we realized that he hadn't actually noticed; which made him all the sweeter for the faith he placed in us.

My anxiety receded, prospects beckoned. Bingo became palatable, or maybe not quite that, but certainly no more hostile than Scrabble. And then we drove back to Toronto, because Allistair had a friend who needed to hire a coordinator for the Toronto Jazz Festival, which gave Calvin the notion that he could book fiercely admired appliance players from Amsterdam and Berlin and at the same time assemble his own new band. I didn't argue, for I understood what he needed now. I couldn't ask him to morph into a money-earning man and support me in New York. I'd get back to my beloved city somehow, to my Tristan, but not yet. A deeper love and more focused ambition would unfurl above the treeline.

As we packed the car, Bernice fell into a crumpled, tearful heap on her front lawn while Stan waggled his eyebrows and chuckled.

"You hate Cape Breton," she wailed. "You'll never come back!"

"Your mother truly is as crazy as a shithouse rat," I said to Calvin.

"And you are not?" he asked me, sidelong.

"Holy shit, Calvin." Did he love me because of her, because he was used to a woman like her? "I am *nothing* like your mother!" I whispered hotly, cuffing him in the head.

"I was *joking*," he said, protecting himself with his hands and laughing. "You're supposed to take me away from this, don't you get it? You're the mama in my family now. You're the mama."

We assured Bernice that our departure wasn't a rejection of New Waterford, not at all, please. Please stop crying. It was just for the time being. Life is like that, always lived for the time being. One tentative agreement to go forward, and then another. I took Calvin's hand, and walked across the grass with my son upon my hip.

My love is my weight, wrote St. Augustine. *Because of it I move.*

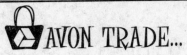

AVON TRADE...

because every great bag deserves a great book!

BARE NECESSITY
by Carole Matthews
0-06-053214-9 • $13.95 US

THE SECOND COMING OF LUCY HATCH
by Marsha Moyer
0-06-008166-X • $13.95 US • $21.95 Can

DOES SHE OR DOESN'T SHE?
by Alisa Kwitney
0-06-051237-7• $13.95 US • $21.95 Can

LOVE AND A BAD HAIR DAY
by Annie Flannigan
0-380-81936-8• $13.95 US • $21.95 Can

GET SOME LOVE
by Nina Foxx
0-06-052648-3• $13.95 US • $21.95 Can

A GIRL'S BEST FRIEND
by Elizabeth Young
0-06-056277-3 • $13.95 US

RULES FOR A PRETTY WOMAN
by Suzette Francis
0-06-053542-3 • $13.95 US • $21.95 Can

THE NANNY
by Melissa Nathan
0-06-056011-8 • $13.95 US

ALWAYS TRUE TO YOU IN MY FASHION
by Valerie Wilson Wesley
0-06-054942-4 • $13.95 US • $21.95 Can

PLAYING HOUSE
by Patricia Pearson
0-06-053437-0 • $13.95 US